# "So, you're out here to hunt a husband?"

"There are other possibilities for a woman now besides marriage." Lacey's voice rang with a soft, inner conviction.

The flash of surprise in Holt's metallic eyes was barely concealed, and not before Lacey caught a glimpse of something else. Disapproval?

"What you're looking for shouldn't be too hard to find." He gritted out the words with deceptive gentleness.

"You misunderstand, Holt," Lacey told him with seething calm. "I'm looking for a relationship that, when the excitement fades, can be terminated without bitterness."

"You're talking about becoming some man's mistress?" he retorted gruffly.

"I'm talking about a totally equal arrangement. There will be no question of being any man's kept woman!"

"So you're going to indulge yourself in a series of affairs?" he asked derisively.

"Why not? I think it's time I find out what I've been missing...."

# STEPHANIE JAMES

is a pseudonym for bestselling, award-winning author **Jayne Ann Krentz**. Under various pseudonyms—including Jayne Castle and Amanda Quick—Ms. Krentz has over 22 million copies of her books in print. Her fans admire her versatility as she switches between historical, contemporary and futuristic romances. She attributes a "lifelong addiction to romantic daydreaming" as the chief influence on her writing. With her husband, Frank, she currently resides in the Pacific Northwest.

## JAYNE ANN KRENTZ
### WRITING AS

# Stephanie James

## VELVET
## TOUCH

# Silhouette Books

**Published by Silhouette Books**
**America's Publisher of Contemporary Romance**

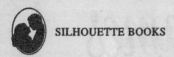

**SILHOUETTE BOOKS**

ISBN 0-373-80667-1

VELVET TOUCH

Copyright © 1982 by Jayne Ann Krentz

This edition published by arrangement with Harlequin Books S.A.

**Printed in U.S.A.**

# One

"You're crazy!"

The words echoed in Lacey Seldon's ears as she guided the snappy red Fiat off the Washington State Ferry and up the ramp to the lush, green island which was to be her home for the summer.

She'd been hearing those words or similar ones for the past three months, ever since she'd exploded the bomb of her decision. The shock waves were probably still ricocheting around the Iowa cornfields, reverberating through the small, midwestern university town where she had been born and raised and where she had lived every one of her twenty-nine years.

"You're crazy!"

Everyone had told her that. The head librarian had said it in his kindly, paternalistic manner when she had handed in her resignation as chief of the Reference Department.

Her parents had said it, her mother in tears, when she gave them the news. Her father the banker and her brother the stockbroker had taken the rational, economic approach:

"Leave a good job just when you're in line for another promotion? Don't be an idiot, Lacey!"

"You haven't even got another job to go to! At least wait until you've found something else!"

"Take the money left over from the sale of your house and live on that? But that should be set aside for the future! You may need it for something really important some day!"

Her mother's arguments, predictably enough, were more emotional. In that respect they were probably more honest. She, at least, was saying the things everyone else was really thinking.

"But you can't move away! You've lived here all your life. This is where you belong. Why won't you be sensible and marry that nice professor of psychology? You'd make a wonderful mother for his two sweet children.

"Why are you doing this? You've never been a…a wild sort of girl. You were always so well behaved, such a source of pride to your father and me." And then, more thoughtfully, "Except for the divorce, of course. But everyone knows that wasn't your fault. Besides, that was over two years ago, mercifully. You've had plenty of time to get over it. You don't belong out there on the West Coast. You know the sort of people who live out there. You've always been such a *nice* girl!''

The yard sale had been the largest in the town's history. Nobody ever moved and so such events tended to be on a small scale. But Lacey lined up nearly all her worldly possessions beneath the huge shade tree in the front yard. The house itself had been sold two weeks earlier and she was moving out as soon as her things were disposed of.

Everyone came, naturally, mostly out of curiosity. But it made for a very profitable sale. Aunt Selma, the one who had never married, took a look at the avidly interested crowd pawing through Lacey's things and winked at her niece. She had been the only one to show some understanding of Lacey's decision. Lacey wondered if it was because the woman might possibly remember what it felt like to be turning thirty and be trapped in a small town where everyone knew what was best for you.

''I'll take your mother home for a cup of coffee,'' Selma had announced firmly. ''She'll never make it through this day without collapsing in hysteria if I don't!''

Lacey's mother, however, had survived, just as Lacey had known she would. The descendants of the strong, proud women who had made the Midwest into the heartland of America were basically made of very stern stuff. When Lacey finally found herself standing beside the packed Fiat, her family grouped loyally on the sidewalk in front of the home where she had been born, it was Mrs. Seldon who said with sudden decision, "You know, dear, I think that charming professor might not have been quite right for you after all. Imagine anyone who doesn't believe children should be given a sound wallop now and again! Perhaps there will be someone waiting for you out there on the West Coast...."

Mrs. Seldon was a practical woman. Lacey was almost thirty years old. She needed a husband and if she wasn't going to settle down with anyone locally, then the search had better be extended beyond the borders of town.

Lacey had kissed them all: her mother, her aunt, her brother and her father. They had each told her to write frequently, to be careful, and to remember where home was. And for the first time since she had made the decision, Lacey herself had cried. She'd climbed into the overstuffed Fiat and had barely been able to see through the windshield because of the moisture in her eyes.

But the tears had dried by the time she'd reached the Iowa border. She wasn't crazy, Lacey told herself with an inner smile of satisfaction. In fact, this was probably the first sane thing she'd done in a life which had been a series of proper, conventional events since the day of her birth.

All the way through the Midwest and across the Mountain states she had thought about the beautiful, green island in the San Juan chain off the coast of Washington. It drew her like a magnet, symbolizing the complete change of direction she was making in her own life. It would be the starting point for a decade which Lacey Seldon had determined would not be as wasted as the last one had been.

So many years, she thought now as she followed the signs along a narrow road which encircled the island. So many years wasted. Her twenties. The years when she should be seeing the world, finding a fascinating job, discovering the unknown, taking risks, and perhaps finding out what real romance and passion could be. All that time gone with nothing to show for it but a broken marriage, a job which had become incredibly routine, and no prospects of ever finding the exciting side of life.

But this summer she, Lacey Seldon, would take charge of her own life and change all that. The restlessness which had been growing steadily until it had peaked in her twenty-ninth year had finally become more clamoring than all the rational arguments for continuing with her safe, monotonous life-style. Lacey Seldon was determined that her thirties would not be a repeat of the wasted years of her twenties. Life was short. Finally, before it was too late, she was going to *live!*

The small map on the back of the brochure which had been sent to her by the inn seemed accurate enough. The winding road slipped beneath the wheels of the Fiat, towering pines on one side, sweeping views of Puget Sound on the other.

Eventually the small sign announcing the turnoff came into view and Lacey swung the little car around the corner, following an even narrower road as it curved along the edge of a quiet little bay.

There, nestled cozily on the shore, was the Randolph Inn. Lacey smiled. It looked exactly as it had in the brochure. A huge veranda wrapped around the second level, rows of French doors opening out onto it. Stone and thick cedar logs had been used in the construction of a building which had been designed during an era of old-fashioned graciousness. In front of the main lodge a wide lawn stretched to the shore where small waves lapped lazily. Behind the main building she could see the tiny cottages snugly fitted into the pine and fir trees. One of those was hers.

Lacey parked the car in the tiny lot, pulled off the scarf which had kept her shoulder-length auburn hair in place in the open car and shook the deep, fiery tresses free. She had been growing her hair for the past two years, although few had noticed the small indication of incipient rebellion because she'd habitually worn the soft mass in a businesslike knot at the back of her head.

But today, as it had during the entire week's drive, Lacey's hair swung freely about her shoulders, falling in a graceful wave from the simple center part.

It framed a pair of auburn-lashed blue-green eyes which tilted upward very slightly at the corners. The eyes were full of intelligence, ready humor, and not a little of that strong, midwestern stubbornness which had helped create a mighty nation.

The rest of the face, Lacey thought with typical realism, couldn't be classed as more than reasonably attractive. The problem with the face, she had long since decided, was that it didn't have either the cute, elfin charm or the sexy, seething look which would have gone so well with the deep red hair. The combination of a firmly etched nose, high cheekbones, and a mouth that smiled easily was not unattractive but the overall impression tended to be one of wholesomeness rather than outright sensuality.

But there were ways of camouflaging that sort of look she had decided. And one of them was with clothes. As she stepped from the Fiat, the yellow, crinkled gauze cloud of a dress swirled about her slender figure, its very drifting quality somehow calling attention to the small, high breasts and gracefully rounded hips. Together with the strappy sandals on her bare feet and the outrageous hoop earrings, it gave her a cheerful, free-spirited look, she thought.

She snatched up the huge, floppy shoulder bag and walked toward the main entrance of the lodge. It was one of those sunny summer days the San Juans boasted of and several guests were lazing above her on the veranda, icy drinks in their hands. Somewhere, she knew from careful reading of the brochure, there was an indoor-outdoor pool.

The lobby was empty when she stepped through the open French doors, no one waiting helpfully behind the antique front desk. Tentatively she rang the little bell, glancing around expectantly. When no one appeared after another moment, she shrugged and walked over to gaze out the window. She was in no hurry. She had the rest of her life ahead of her.

That thought was shaping her lips into a small, secret little smile when a deep, gravely polite voice spoke from behind her. "I'm sorry, miss, but I'm afraid the inn is full. Unless you have a reservation…?" The tone of the dark, rough velvet voice said clearly that he didn't think she did.

"I do," Lacey hastened to assure him, swinging around to confront the man standing in the doorway behind the desk. He was leaning against the jamb, idly wiping his hands on a white towel. And, somehow, he didn't look at all as she had expected a desk clerk to look. But she was out West now. Folks were bound to be different out here.

The smile which had been edging her lips widened brightly as she bent her head to dig about in the large shoulder bag. "I've got the confirmation somewhere in here. I'm renting one of the cottages for the summer, not a room in the inn, itself."

"But all the cottages have been reserved and the tenants have arrived, except for..." He broke off, a strange, slightly startled expression flickering in his silvery haze eyes. "You're not L. Seldon, the librarian from Iowa, are you?"

Lacey gave him a serene, confident glance. "I'm afraid so. Don't fret, you don't look much like what I imagined a desk clerk would look like, either!"

He stared at her and then a slow, answering grin quirked the corners of a rather hard mouth. When the smile reached his eyes, she realized he was concentrating a little too much on the yellow gauze dress. Belatedly Lacey stepped away from the window, ruefully aware of how the sunlight must have been illuminating her figure beneath the thin, summery dress. Firmly she handed him the reservation confirmation.

When he bent his head to scan it briefly, Lacey took the opportunity to study him in more detail.

He must have been around thirty-seven or thirty-eight, she decided analytically, trying to ascertain

just why he hadn't seemed the clerk type. He
looked his age, the years having marked him with
the indefinable quality called experience. But whatever the experience had consisted of, it had not had
a decadent effect. Rather, there was a hardness in
him which spoke silently of a formidable will.

Tawny brown hair was combed carelessly back
from a broad forehead. The thick locks were worn
a little longer than they would have been among
men his age back home, nearly brushing the collar
of his blue work shirt in back. His sleeves had been
rolled up on sinewy, tanned forearms and the shirt
was open at the throat, revealing the beginning of
an equally tanned, hair-roughened chest. Broad
shoulders tapered to a lean, narrow waist. Strong
thighs were sheathed in a pair of close-fitting jeans
which Lacey's mother would have severely
frowned upon. Jeans like that on a man his age? It
wasn't proper! Lacey's laughter gleamed in her
eyes.

When he tossed down the towel and came to
stand directly behind the desk, she saw that a look
of lean, hard strength was clearly stamped on his
face. It was there in the fiercely chiseled planes of
commanding cheekbones, aggressive nose, and un-
yielding chin. It was not a countenance one would
call handsome, yet the impression it gave of authority and quiet power was surprisingly attractive.

He glanced up and saw her watching him and his

silvery hazel eyes flashed with a look of satisfied amusement. He *enjoyed* her scrutiny!

"Welcome, Miss Seldon. We've been expecting you. And so, apparently, have a number of other people!"

She tilted her head in polite inquiry and watched as he ducked down out of sight behind the desk. When he straightened a moment later he was holding a huge, carefully bound stack of mail in his hand.

"We did as you instructed in your letter, Miss Seldon," he informed her politely. "We held all mail for your arrival. It started pouring in about a week ago."

"Oh, good," she murmured, reaching out to take the large stack with an eager hand. "I'm off to a solid start, at least."

"You intend to spend the summer corresponding?" he remarked dryly.

"I intend to spend the summer job hunting." She chuckled, flipping happily through the long white envelopes. "Most of these are from people I've been sending out résumés to for the past couple of months. I used the inn for the return address."

"I see," he said a little blankly. "How many résumés did you send out?"

"Hundreds," she confided cheerily. "With any luck, you'll be getting mail for me all summer long!"

"You've come all the way out here just to job-hunt?" He looked genuinely bewildered, Lacey decided indulgently.

"I've come all the way out here to do a great deal more than that," she assured him soothingly. "Now, shouldn't I sign in somewhere?"

Without a word he slid a form across the polished wood countertop and handed her a pen. He stood silently while she scribbled in the necessary information but she could feel those assessing hazel eyes on her bent head. She wondered what he'd say when he realized she'd put down the inn's address for "current" address.

When she finished he handed her the key and started out from behind the desk. "I'll help you unload the car," he told her.

"You're the chief bellhop as well as desk clerk?" She smiled, leading the way toward the red Fiat.

"I'm afraid so. At least for today. My assistant isn't feeling well," he explained easily. "My name's Randolph, by the way. Holt Randolph. I...uh...own this place."

"Do you?" Lacey remarked, a little surprised, although it did explain why he hadn't struck her as a clerk. "How interesting. How long have you had it?"

He flicked a speculative glance down at her as he paced beside her across the lawn. He must have stood nearly six feet, she thought, feeling a little overwhelmed as he dwarfed her own five feet four inches.

"I inherited it," he said slowly, "from my grandparents."

"Oh." Lacey nodded. "I understand. I didn't realize you people out here did things like that, though."

"Have grandparents?"

"No." She laughed. "Passed businesses down through generations. I thought everyone out here went off on his own early in life to find himself or herself."

"Sometimes we do," he admitted gently, halting beside the little car and raking his eyes over the stuffed interior. "And sometimes we find out that it isn't necessary to abandon everything in order to discover where we belong."

Lacey glanced up at him sharply. She could well believe he was the sort of man who had always known what he wanted. Holt Randolph had that inner sureness which indicated a man who took what he wished from life. The only surprising thing, to her way of thinking, was that he would have wanted to run an old-fashioned inn tucked away on the edge of a tiny island.

"Well, each to his own," she returned breezily, sliding in behind the wheel as he held the tiny door open for her.

"Is that an old midwestern philosophy?" He grinned.

"Are you kidding? One of the reasons I'm out here is to be among people who really do practice that philosophy! Now, which cabin is mine?"

"The one at the top of that small rise. You'll have a view of the Sound from there and plenty of privacy. I'll meet you up there...." he added. "You obviously don't have room to give me a lift!"

Lacey laughed happily, her hand sweeping out in a gentle arc to indicate the boxes piled high even in the passenger seat. "You are viewing all my worldly possessions. I feel like those people on the old wagon trains must have felt when they packed what they could and sold off everything else!"

Holt stared at her for a second and she could see the mingled astonishment and curiosity mirrored in those perceptive hazel eyes. A thousand questions had suddenly leaped to life there and Lacey could have given a shout of sheer satisfaction. Back in Iowa no one had suddenly been consumed with curiosity about her. Everyone knew her, knew her family, and knew her life history. The only time curiosity had been aroused was when people found out she was leaving town.

But Holt merely nodded and started up the path which led toward her cabin. She switched on the ignition and put the Fiat in gear.

She reached the little cottage a minute or so

ahead of him and hurried to unlock the front door, eager for a glimpse of the rustic charm promised in the brochure.

She stepped through the doorway and glanced around expectantly. Yes, it was exactly as promised. Heavy cedar logs framed a cozy little parlor, complete with her own stone hearth. Wide windows on either side of the door provided the view of the main lodge and Puget Sound. A small, compact kitchen occupied a corner of the room and beyond that a hallway extended toward what must be the bedroom and bath.

"Will it do?" her host asked politely, walking up to stand behind her as she took in her new home.

"It's perfect," she told him enthusiastically.

"Some of the furniture's a little ancient, he said somewhat apologetically, his eyes on the quaint, comfortable, overstuffed sofa and lounge chair. "But the bed is new and the bath was redone during the winter...."

"I'm sure it will be fine," she said quickly, wondering why a landlord would sound so apologetic about his property. "It looks just as it did in the brochure."

Thick, braided rugs covered wide sections of the hardwood floor and the curtains were a bright, cheerful print. The sunlight pouring in through the windows reflected warmly off the cedar walls.

"Good, I'm glad you like it," Holt said, appearing somewhat relieved for no apparent reason. "I'll start getting your things in from the car."

"Thank you."

Lacey set down the huge stack of mail on a small desk which had been placed in front of a window and stepped back outside to help unload.

"Were you kidding when you said this lot really does comprise all your worldly belongings?" Holt finally broke down to ask as he lifted her stereo out of the trunk.

"Nope. That's it. I had one of the largest yard sales ever seen in the state of Iowa before I left! I even sold the yard, itself," she added smugly, following him into the cottage with a suitcase in one hand.

He carefully set the stereo down on a low coffee table. "Where are you planning on moving after you've had your summer vacation here?"

"Haven't the foggiest," Lacey said lightly. "We'll have to see what happens this summer. As I said, I'm job hunting and there are several things I intend to do before I decide where to settle next. For now, this is home."

He stood for a moment, watching her as she came through the doorway behind him. The gauze dress swirled around her, caught by a playful breeze. "You know, I hate to say this because I don't believe in stereotypes, but frankly, you just don't look like the small-town librarian we were expecting."

"Good."

"What does the 'L' stand for, anyway?"

"Lacey." She smiled, stepping once more out of the revealing sunlight. She was uncomfortably aware of the faint warmth in her cheeks. Holt Randolph hadn't bothered to disguise his purely male interest in what was outlined by the sun. She wondered if that sort of outright perusal was typical of men out here. Back in Iowa... She cut off that thought briskly. Back in Iowa she would never have worn this dress!

"And you," she went on crisply, "don't look like the sort of person I imagined would be running this place. So much for stereotypes, I suppose!"

"Don't I?" This appeared to amuse him. His eyes gleamed for an instant. "What sort of man do I look like?"

Lacey tilted her head to one side, studying him with mock attention. "Well, I can imagine you running a cattle ranch or working on an offshore oil rig or..."

"Actually," drawled a new voice behind her, "Randolph's very good at what he does, aren't you, Holt? A born innkeeper!"

Lacey whirled in surprise to find a lanky, brown-haired young man with warm brown eyes and a jaunty mustache standing on the path.

"And you must be the librarian he promised! Hi. I'm your next-door neighbor for the summer, Jeremy Todd." He thrust forward the box of unopened painting supplies he had just removed from her trunk. "Are you an artist, too?"

"Hello, I'm Lacey Seldon, and as for being an artist, I don't know," she told him cheerfully, taking the package of new paints and brushes. "I've never tried it. It's something I intend to find out this summer."

"Good afternoon, Todd," Holt said quietly, coming up behind Lacey with a silence that made her start slightly when he spoke. "I see you're not wasting any time."

"When I saw that car, I decided there might be more to our little midwesterner than you had indicated," Jeremy Todd retorted smoothly.

Lacey blinked, disconcerted by the tiny element of masculine hostility which seemed to have entered the atmosphere. Didn't these two men like each other? Surely they weren't reacting so coolly to one another because of her? She had only just arrived, for heaven's sake!

"I bought the car two months ago," she rushed in to say chattily, telling herself the slight chill in the air was purely her imagination. "Everybody in town thought I was nuts. None of the local mechanics knew for sure how to work on it!"

Jeremy grinned, a charming, boyish grin that

went well with his casual jeans and red T-shirt. "Are all the librarians back in Iowa like you?"

"No," Lacey retorted, getting a bit irked by the constant reference to the image of her profession. "Some are blond."

Holt chuckled approvingly. "Come on, Todd. If you're going to hang around Lacey's front door, you might as well make yourself useful. There's a lot of stuff squirreled away in that Fiat."

"Always glad to lend a hand," Jeremy said promptly and followed Holt out the door.

With both men assisting her, it wasn't long before Lacey had her belongings piled neatly around the floor of the cottage. "I think that does it," she observed gratefully. "I really appreciate the help."

"No problem," Hold responded politely, eyeing the small collection with a curious frown. "That's really everything, hmmm?"

"Everything I own in the world." Lacey's look was one of satisfaction as she followed his glance.

"You must have left an awful lot behind in Iowa," he murmured.

"I left twenty-nine years behind in Iowa," she replied with a hint of grimness.

"Going back to them someday?" he asked.

For an instant they met each other's gaze across the room, ignoring Jeremy Todd, who glanced at them both in bewilderment.

"Never."

Holt nodded slowly and Lacey felt herself grow vaguely uneasy beneath the intensity of his eyes. She turned brightly to Jeremy.

"Which cottage is yours?"

"The one right across the way," he said quickly, eager to get back into the conversation. "And if you're not doing anything else this evening, I'll be glad to show you just how much at home Randolph is in his line of work?"

"What do you mean?"

"Jeremy's referring to the way we spend the evenings up at the lodge," Holt interposed swiftly, seeing her confusion. "The folks in the cottages are welcome to join us, of course."

"There's an after-dinner brandy hour in front of the fireplace and then dancing in the lounge," Jeremy explained. "You can watch Randolph mingle with the guests. He's really quite good at it. Everyone looks forward to the evenings around here. Want to come along? I'll be going up around eight."

Lacey stifled the sensation of being rushed. Of course she wanted to go. It would be an excellent start to the summer. "Thanks, I'd like that," she said with a smile.

"I'll see you both later this evening, then," Holt said in a slightly formal tone of voice as he turned abruptly and made for the door. "Call the office if you need anything, Lacey."

Lacey watched him disappear down the path toward the lodge, inwardly curious at her own reaction to the sight of his lean, catlike stride. There was a certain male grace in his movement. Strange, she had never really thought about a man's way of walking before. Jeremy's voice called back her wandering attention.

"Need any help putting all this stuff away?" he inquired, inspecting her collection of flamenco records.

"No, thanks. I'll want to think about how to organize it." She hesitated. "Will people be dressing up for this evening?" she finally asked.

"No, we keep things pretty casual around here. Something like what you have on will be fine," he added, giving the sheer yellow dress the same sort of glance it had received from Holt.

"That's a relief. I mean, I've always heard people out here were fairly casual but when one's never been in Rome before it's hard to second-guess...."

"A pair of jeans and a swimsuit will see you through the summer," he said with a grin.

"Those I've got! Are you going to be here all summer, too?"

"Yes." He gave her a somewhat sheepish, rather hopeful glance. "I'm going to try and write a book."

"That's great! What kind of book?" Lacey was an old hand at encouraging such projects. A great portion of her career as a librarian was spent in assisting people who were in the process of creating papers, books, and articles. Librarians learned early that such people thrived on a little demonstrated interest.

"It's one of those men's adventure novels. You know, lots of intrigue, a bit of sex, and the old macho ingredients."

"Your first?" she hazarded perceptively.

"Yeah." His mouth twisted wryly. "I'm trying to get out of the insurance business."

Lacey smiled in deepest sympathy. "I understand. Believe me. It would appear we're both going to spend the summer looking for new careers!"

Jeremy's eyes warmed happily. "You, too?"

"Uh-huh. New career and a new life. I'm going to use this inn as a base of operations for the summer. It seems like just the place to plan a fresh start."

Jeremy smiled broadly. "Something tells me we're going to find a lot in common, Lacey Seldon."

Lacey smiled back. A lot more in common than she would ever find with a man like Holt Randolph, she decided privately. The sort of man who was content to take over a family-owned business and make it his life, the sort of man who had probably never wanted anything else except to run this inn; no, she would have nothing very much in common with such a man.

# *Two*

"The inn is the most popular night spot on the island during the summer," Jeremy told Lacey as they walked into the inviting lobby. A fire blazed merrily on the hearth of the huge stone fireplace which dominated one end of the room; several guests were lounging about comfortably, brandy in hand. Nights in the San Juans could be chilly.

"Because it's the only night spot on the island?" Lacey hazarded as Holt Randolph glanced up from his conversation with an elderly woman near the fire.

Jeremy laughed. "How did you guess? Many of the people who show up later on for the dancing will be from private cottages and motels in the area.

It makes for a fairly lively crowd. Ah! We've been spotted. Here comes the brandy."

Holt was making his way toward them, every inch the charming host as far as Lacey could determine. He was wearing a summer-weight linen jacket in a fine light blue pinstripe. Dark blue slacks and a crisp white shirt went together nicely to give him a casually elegant look. In one hand he carried a bottle of expensive brandy and two small glasses.

The smile was for both herself and Jeremy, Lacey guessed, but she knew the swift, appraising glance was directed at her alone. In spite of Jeremy's admonition not to worry about her clothes, she was glad she'd stopped in Seattle long enough to replace some of the wardrobe she'd sold at the yard sale.

Tonight was the first chance she'd had to wear the exotically patterned silk dress from India. Worn belted at the waist, it drifted around her knees. The look was satisfyingly casual and rich in an understated way. The jewel-toned blues and greens complimented the dark fire of her hair and reflected the color of her eyes. She saw the flash of pleasure in Holt's expression and wondered why it pleased her.

"I'm glad you could make it," he said suavely, handing her and Jeremy a glass and pouring brandy. "Jeremy, you've been here a week and know the routine. I'll leave you on your own while I introduce Lacey."

"I can do that..." Jeremy started to say but Lacey found herself whisked out of earshot before the protest could be completed.

"One of the few privileges of being in charge around here," Holt murmured by way of explanation, one hand locked firmly under her arm. "The boy's too young for you, anyway," he added outrageously.

"I'll be thirty this summer, Mr. Randolph," Lacey retorted coolly. "At my age a woman starts appreciating younger men!" Never in a million years would she have made a remark like that to a near-stranger back in Iowa, she thought happily.

He cocked one tawny brow, turning his head to look down at her. "Surely even back in the Midwest women have learned the value of the...er... vintage stuff over the brashness of younger material!"

Lacey drew a small breath. She wasn't accustomed to this sort of conversation with a man she'd just met. But if that was the way they did things out here...

"I came out West to find variety, Mr. Randolph, not to prove the wisdom of old adages."

He brought her to a halt in front of the fireplace and his mouth twisted sardonically as he watched her sip his brandy. "You're determined to leave all the old ways behind?" he inquired softly.

"All of them."

"Does that include a man?"

"I don't think that's really any of your business," Lacey said calmly, growing uneasily aware of the intensity of that silvery gaze. It seemed to spark a curious response in her, a kind of excitement that went beyond that normally produced in a mild flirtation.

But that must be what it was, she told herself placatingly. A flirtation. Her second since arriving, if she counted Jeremy. Life was looking up. And, while she had determined that Holt Randolph didn't represent what she was searching for now in a man, the practice couldn't hurt.

"I only wanted to be prepared in case some irate male shows up on my doorstep and accuses me of harboring a runaway wife," Holt assured her.

"You're quite safe. There's no husband to come running after me. He left me willingly and everyone else back there thinks I've gone crazy," she admitted with a grin.

"Have you?"

"I prefer to think I escaped before I actually did go crazy!"

"Sure you're not just on the rebound from the missing husband?"

"Do you always get this personal with your guests?" she returned chillingly.

"Only the ones who interest me," he said smoothly.

She hesitated, debating about whether or not to answer the compelling look in his eyes. Then, with a tiny shrug she decided to outline things for him. What did it matter?

"You needn't fret. I'm not exactly on the rebound from the divorce. It was over two years ago. Right after I'd finished paying off the last of his medicalschool bills. He married another doctor. Said he needed someone with whom he had something in common," she explained briefly. "And I don't think you need worry about Harold, either," she added reflectively, openly mocking.

He grimaced. "I'm going to hate myself for asking, but who's Harold?"

"Harold is a professor of psychology at the university where I worked," she told him breezily, marveling at how easily she was adapting to the bantering conversation. She couldn't possibly have joked about poor Harold back in Iowa. Everyone knew him. "He asked me to marry him this past spring. I fit the profile," she explained dramatically.

"This is like sinking into quicksand. What profile?"

"The strong, earth-mother type." Lacey chuckled, remembering Harold and his little inkblots. "Which is kind of funny when you stop to consider that I'm not overly fond of children and his two kids brought out the most aggressive tendencies in me. I wanted to swat them both on more than one occasion. He's raising them very carefully according to some advanced psychology. The day I told him they needed a good wallop instead of an encounter session he withdrew his offer of marriage.''

She saw the smile lurking in Holt's eyes and sighed ruefully. ''Another shot at a good marriage down the tubes. I'm not sure mom will ever forgive me. And time's running out, you know,'' she told him wisely. ''I have it on the best authority that after thirty a woman's chances go down rapidly.''

''And whose authority would that be?''

''Aunt Selma. She turned down the traveling salesman who came through town when she was twenty-nine. It was her last opportunity, she told me. She's wanted to kick herself ever since.''

''So you're out here to hunt a husband along with a new job?'' Holt demanded carefully, taking another sip of his brandy.

''Fortunately the options have widened since my aunt was twenty-nine.'' Lacey's voice lost its bantering quality and rang with soft, inner conviction. ''There are other possibilities for a woman now besides marriage. I've been offered marriage twice and I'm not terribly impressed with the institution. The first time my hand was requested because it represented a meal ticket. I made the classic mistake of working to put my husband through his last years of medical training and internship. He'd run out of money the year he met me. The second opportunity for wedded bliss occurred because I fit some stupid profile of motherhood. Thank heavens I had more sense by then. The next time I become involved with a man, it will be strictly a matter of romance and passion. No strings attached and no hidden bargains!''

The flash of surprise in the metallic eyes was barely concealed and not before Lacey caught a glimpse of something else. Disapproval? She bit her lip in a small, unconscious gesture of self-condemnation. What was she doing standing here and giving this man her life's story? She'd better cut back on the brandy!

But it was too late to retrench now. Holt jumped in with both feet, his censure plain.

''What you're looking for shouldn't be too hard to find,'' he gritted with deceptive gentleness. ''Is Jeremy Todd the first man slated to experience the all-new you?''

The only thing to do was brazen out the rest of the discussion, Lacey decided with an inner sigh. She might as well take the opportunity of letting Holt Randolph know she hadn't come all this way just to find more of the sort of disapproval and advice she could have gotten for free back home!

''I haven't decided yet,'' she said in liquid accents. ''Jeremy and I are just getting to know one another and I want to be quite sure...''

''Sure! Sure about what?'' he rasped heatedly,

forcing Lacey to wonder what was riling him. He might not find her future plans suitable in his estimation but she was, after all, only one of his summer guests. "Why concern yourself with being 'sure' at all?" Holt went on in a cold drawl. "You can always scratch an unsuccessful experiment and start over if things go wrong!"

"You misunderstand, Holt," Lacey told him with a seething calm. "I've given this a great deal of thought. I'm looking for an interesting, reasonably long-lasting relationship which, when the excitement fades, can be terminated without the bitterness of divorce...."

"You're talking about becoming some man's mistress?" he shot back gruffly, taking a rather large gulp of his brandy.

That annoyed her and Lacey frowned at him severely. "I'm talking about a totally equal arrangement. Don't forget all those letters from potential employers you were saving for me. I will support myself. There will be no question of being any man's kept woman!"

"So you're going to indulge yourself in a series of affairs?" he asked derisively.

"Why not? I found out what the traditional marriage has to offer during the years when I should have been learning about real romance. I spent twenty-nine years putting up with the values of small-town life. Now I'm going to make up for what I missed!''

"Oh, my God,'' he breathed, looking appalled. "You're going to go through a midlife crisis right here at my inn!''

Lacey relaxed, the smile shaping her mouth full of pure, feminine taunting. She liked that appalled look on him. It reminded her of all the appalled expressions she had left behind and it gave her a singular pleasure to add fuel to the fire. "Why not? I took one look at the brochure you sent me and decided this island looked like the ideal place to go through such a crisis.'' Turning on her heel she walked off to find Jeremy Todd.

The smile was still mirrored in her eyes an hour later when Lacey slipped into Jeremy's arms on the dance floor. Her hand rested lightly on the shoulder of his corduroy jacket and he encircled her waist with an increasingly familiar touch.

"You were right. This place does seem to be the bright spot of the island's nightlife,'' she said, glancing at the number of people filling the lounge. Many, she knew, were not staying at the Randolph Inn.

"I'm devoted to my new career as a writer but I didn't want to go overboard in isolating myself. This place has a reputation for being lively during the summer months but still provides peace and quiet if one wants it. And we're not too far from

Seattle or Vancouver. If a person gets island fever there's always the brief escape.'' Jeremy grinned.

''I intend to see those cities while I'm in the area,'' she agreed.

''If you're job hunting around the Northwest, you'll have plenty of opportunities...'' he began, not understanding.

''This is only a base for my job hunting,'' she emphasized. ''I've got applications and résumés out all up and down the entire West Coast and in Hawaii. There's no telling where I'll finally end up. I'd say the odds are probably in California, though. But I'm in no rush. I have the summer to see the Northwest.''

''You mean you might be leaving for California or Hawaii?'' Jeremy asked curiously.

''This summer is only the extended vacation I've been promising myself.''

''I see.'' His boyish grin returned. ''I hope you don't have anything against summer romances?''

''I don't know.'' She smiled. ''I've never really had one!''

''You've been missing something.''

''I know.''

He pulled her closer as the music flowed around them and Lacey didn't resist. He was nice, she told herself. And she thought they understood each other very well.

She listened attentively as he talked about the hero he was developing for his novel.

"I'm hoping to sell it to one of the publishing houses which puts out series books," Jeremy explained.

"And if it doesn't sell right away?" she queried sympathetically.

"Then it's back to the insurance business in the fall." He groaned.

On the way back to their small table in the dimly lit lounge, Jeremy stopped and introduced her to some of the guests he had already met.

"I didn't notice Randolph making good on his claim that he was going to handle introductions." He chuckled wryly as they moved away from a charming middle-aged couple who had the cottage behind Jeremy's. "What was that conversation in front of the fireplace all about, anyway? You sure left him with a frustrated expression on his face!"

"We were discussing my future plans," Lacey said dryly. "I got the impression he doesn't entirely approve. Although why it should matter one way or another to him, I can't imagine."

Her escort laughed, seating her. "It's probably because he had such a firm image of you in his mind before you arrived and you're not fitting it at all!"

Lacey lifted one brow interrogatively. "What image was that? And how did he come to tell you about it?''

"I asked him who was going to have the cottage next to mine and he explained he had a sweet little librarian coming in from the Midwest. I think he wanted to let me know he wasn't going to provide any free summer entertainment of that nature.''

"He does seem a little on the…uh…conservative side,'' Lacey observed vaguely. "I mean, considering the fact that he's single.…'' She broke off as a sudden thought struck her. "He is single, isn't he?''

"He is at the moment. According to the Millers—'' he named the couple to whom he had just introduced Lacey ''—that status may not last long. They've been coming to the inn for years and remember his ex-fiancée very well. She apparently ran off to marry another man and has since divorced. Edith says she hears by the grapevine that the mystery woman from Randolph's past has made reservations here sometime during the summer. Edith and Sam seem to think our host may still be carrying the torch.''

Lacey's eyes lit up. "Fascinating! Maybe he was scorned once by a free-thinking woman in the past and has been hostile toward the species ever since!''

"I don't know all the details.'' Jeremy shrugged, clearly losing interest.

Lacey took the hint and changed the subject with a willing smile. They were deep into a conversation on sailing, one of Jeremy's hobbies and one to which he was volunteering to introduce Lacey, when Holt once again appeared out of the large crowd.

Lacey, for one, wasn't altogether surprised to see him. Out of the corner of her eye she'd caught sight of him dancing with several of his female guests. His attentiveness must make him a very popular host, she decided.

"Join us for a drink, Holt?" Jeremy asked casually, glancing up as the other man came to a halt beside the small table. Lacey noted the cool politeness between the two men and smiled to herself.

"Thanks, but I'm making my social rounds. Lacey here is next on the list. If you'll excuse us...?" Holt turned to pin Lacey with a smile.

"Just remember to bring her back," Jeremy grinned cheerfully. "We're in the middle of a very interesting discussion. Did you know the poor, deprived woman has never been on a sailboat in her life?"

"I'm sure they have other ways of occupying their time back there in Iowa," Holt opined reaching down to encircle Lacey's wrist with a grip that felt like a manacle. "Ready, Lacey?" The gleam in his eyes dared her to refuse.

"There's really no need to include me on your

list of duty dances, Holt," she began very firmly, trying unobtrusively to remove her wrist. "I'm being nicely entertained, as you can see."

"But I insist," he countered smoothly, forcing her lightly to her feet with no obvious effort. "I always take my responsibilities very seriously."

Lacey tossed a rueful smile over her shoulder at Jeremy, who grinned in response as she found herself being led off in the direction of the dance floor.

"One dance, Holt. That's all that's necessary," she said in a cool, remote little voice as he drew her into his arms.

"You must let me be the judge of what's necessary and what isn't," he admonished a little grimly as his hand locked around her waist. She could feel the hard warmth of his touch through the delicate Indian silk as he continued his statement. "I have it all down to a fine art, you see."

"Do you dance with all the women who stay here?"

"At least once."

"It's good for business?" she murmured in wry amusement.

"Very good."

Lacey thought about the imminent arrival of his ex-fiancée and knew she had enough feminine curiosity to want to see him dance with the woman from his past. Was he looking forward to the experience? Or would she be the exception to his rule?

"Do you mind some of the social obligations of your job?" she heard herself ask with genuine interest. "You seem to have spent the entire evening mingling. Is that routine?"

He shrugged, somehow managing to maneuver her a few inches closer in the process. She was aware of the feel of his expensive jacket under her fingers and the scent of a spicy aftershave which blended very attractively with the clean maleness of him.

"It's routine, but I don't mind. I want my guests to enjoy themselves. But in this instance..."

"I didn't ask you to dance with me. You're the one who insisted," Lacey reminded him, lifting her chin slightly in the faintest of challenges.

"It's not the dancing I'm finding unpleasant," he countered in a deep drawl. "In fact, you feel quite good in my arms. All silky and light..." He paused as Lacey's eyes narrowed and then continued equably enough, "What I'm not expecting to enjoy is your reaction when I give you the standard lecture on Jeremy Todd."

She groaned, making a face up at him. "You're absolutely right. I don't think I want to hear it. Shall we just agree to skip the whole thing? I'll take your duty as done."

"Sorry, my conscience would bother me for

weeks. The plain truth is, Todd is a nice enough guy but he fancies himself as something of a playboy. He stayed here for a few weeks last summer and I had the unenviable privilege of watching him in action.''

''Don't you think I'm old enough to take care of myself? As I recall, you were telling me earlier he's much too young for me, anyway.'' Lacey lifted one eyebrow baitingly. She should have guessed Holt Randolph would feel obliged to warn her. He was acting like her brother!

''I think,'' he said very distinctly, ''that you're more vulnerable than some women your age might be, Lacey. From what you've told me so far, you've lived a rather sheltered small-town life. Having gone through a divorce doesn't give you any special immunity to men who use women.''

Lacey couldn't resist. ''Perhaps, as I tried to explain in our first conversation this evening, I'm not entirely opposed to being used!''

''I don't think you understand just what you're. saying. Jeremy Todd is looking strictly for a summer affair, and in spite of your newly liberated approach to the subject, it's possible you're still a small-town girl underneath!''

''If there are any vestiges of such a creature still left, I shall be only too happy to get rid of them!''

''Lacey, don't get angry with me. I told you, I'm only doing my duty by warning you about Todd,'' he said coaxingly, a frown of genuine concern connecting the tawny brows.

"Consider it done. Could we please talk about something else for the remainder of the dance?" she responded roundly, her irritation plain in her faintly slanting eyes. The man was beginning to become more annoying than amusing. He would have done very well back in Iowa!

The lines at the edges of Holt's mouth tightened in frustration as he noted the lack of impact being made by his words. "Another topic? Certainly. How about discussing why you chose my inn for your great escape?" he growled.

"Delighted. You should be quite proud. I selected your resort from among hundreds of others all up and down the coast. Yours won out even though it didn't promise a hot tub or a heart-shaped pool in every room!"

"I'm flattered," he grated. "I hadn't realized the competition was getting so tough!"

"I'm afraid I chose your island for other reasons," she went on, ignoring his sarcasm. "I wanted some place that would be a total change from cornfields and university campuses but I also wanted an area that wouldn't overwhelm me at first. You see, Holt?" she adding mockingly. "I've still got a bit of midwestern practicality. This summer is going to be quite a change for me. I want to slip into my new life-style as comfortably as possible.

Your inn represented a place that was both a retreat in some ways and highly accessible in others. From here I can survey my future, and take my time adjusting to my new life-style.''

"You really intend this change to be permanent?" he demanded, searching her upturned features as if looking for serious answers.

"Very permanent," she vowed. "I'm never going back to Iowa. From now on I'm going to take the best and most interesting of what life has to offer. But I'm also sensible enough to realize that plunging too quickly into an alien environment can cause problems. Hence, the decision to start in the Northwest instead of throwing myself right into, say, Southern California." She concluded with a small laugh.

He slanted her an odd glance. "You've done a lot of thinking about this, haven't you?"

"And planning. I'm cursed with a flair for organization," she informed him dryly. "Comes from being a librarian, I suppose."

"Then it would be a shame to see you swept off your feet before you were quite ready for that step in your metamorphosis," he inserted promptly, as if pouncing on an apparent flaw in her thinking. "It would be too bad if you didn't have an opportunity to bring all those plans to fruition on schedule."

"Perhaps being swept off my feet is one of my plans," Lacey retorted agreeably, beginning to enjoy herself. "You know, you'd be right at home back in Iowa. Oh, you'd probably have to cut your hair a bit and make a few other minor adjustments in your attire, but other than that, you'd fit in immediately. My family would love you!"

"Which recommendation is enough to damn me out of hand in your eyes, right?"

"Let's just say that thus far the members of my family haven't proved to be excellent judges of character."

"They all loved the doctor and Harold the psych professor?" he hazarded interestedly.

"I'm afraid so."

"What makes you think I'm in the same category?" he prodded.

"A certain intrinsic, pompous authority," she claimed with relish.

"Pompous!" A slow grin suddenly revealed very white teeth as he considered that. The humor caught fire in the silvery eyes and for the first time Lacey felt a flicker of uncertainty in her assessment. If there was one thing neither her ex-husband nor Harold had been able to do, it was laugh at themselves. "You find me pompous?"

"Wouldn't you think the same of me if I attempted to warn you off another woman within hours of having met you?" she pointed out reasonably.

He sighed ruefully, his hand sliding a little farther down her spine to fit the curve of her waist more intimately. "I might," he suggested slowly, "take it as a sign of interest...."

"Are you interested in me, Holt?" Lacey challenged softly. Was that the reason for his unwarranted warnings? She was suddenly very intrigued.

"You're not quite what I'd expected," he hedged, not denying the charge.

"I know," she acknowledged. "Is that the reason you're so concerned? You're having trouble reconciling the real me with the image you'd built up in your mind based on a rental application?"

"No," he finally admitted reluctantly. He seemed fascinated with the expression in her blue-green eyes. "There are a few other factors involved...."

"For instance?" she invited, knowing she was openly flirting now and taking pleasure in the experience.

He drew a breath as if about to plunge into a cold stream. "You remind me of someone I used to know."

The laughing challenge was wiped from Lacey's eyes in an instant to be replaced by rueful comprehension. "I should have guessed," she said dryly, thinking of the ex-fiancée.

"How could you?" he countered, surprising her. "You didn't meet me when I was in the middle of my own life-style crisis." He chuckled.

"What?" She stared at him, confused. She was sure he had been thinking she was on the verge of becoming a heartless creature like the woman from his past.

"What you're going through reminds me of myself and what I went through a few years ago," he explained gently. "You're not the first to arrive at the earthshaking conclusion that you're missing something critical in life, Lacey Seldon. And you're not the only one to opt for a complete change of life-style in an effort to rectify the situation."

"You're telling me you went through a similar experience?" she asked, eyes widening in disbelief. "I can't quite see you having qualms about yourself or anything else!"

"I don't have them. Not now," he stated evenly.

"But there was a time…?" she pressed, burning with curiosity now.

"Yes. There was a time," he told her quietly, his eyes very serious. "Want to hear what I learned during that time?"

"No!" The single negative almost exploded from her. "I can see what you learned! You decided to stick with the safe and sane path, didn't you? Whatever the degree of crisis you experienced, it doesn't seem to have succeeded in changing your life. Therefore your conclusions are invalid as far as I'm concerned. Because I *am* going to change my world, Holt. And I don't particularly want any lectures from someone who didn't manage to make the break himself!''

''You're not willing to learn from someone else's mistakes?'' he bit out.

''When one is setting out to build a new life, one needs successful role models!''

''Not failures?'' he concluded for her, his voice suddenly harsh.

Lacey shut her eyes briefly and felt the red wash into her cheeks. She would never have been so openly rude under normal circumstances. What was the matter with her? Why was she letting this one man affect her so? Deliberately she took a grip on her temper and looked up at him through her lashes. ''We each have to make our own choices, Holt. You, apparently, have already made yours. And that's your own business. I'm sure you can understand, however, that I don't particularly want you or anyone else making mine for me.''

''Lacey, listen to me....''

''If you'll excuse me, I should be getting back to Jeremy.'' She gave him her most brilliant smile. ''You can rest assured you've done your duty!''

Without waiting for his verbal agreement, Lacey turned away and walked off the dance floor. It occurred to her that this was the second time she'd walked away from him that evening. And she barely knew the man!

## *Three*

She was sitting cross-legged on a mat, palms
curved upward as her hands rested on her knees,
facing the rising sun the next morning when Holt
Randolph again intruded.

"A meditation freak? Perhaps you do belong out
here, Lacey. I can imagine that sort of thing was
rather frowned upon back home, wasn't it?" His
voice was dry but there was an underlying humor
which found a response in her.

"Good morning, Holt," Lacey said calmly, not
bothering to open her eyes. She knew he was directly behind her, could feel him studying her figure
as she sat on a mat which she'd placed at a strategic
point on the lawn behind the cottage. "Just stop-

ping by to see whether or not Jeremy spent the
night? You remind me of a dorm mother I once had
in college. Now that you've seen I'm all alone
you'd best hurry on to the next cottage. No telling
what exciting activities the occupants might be up
to there!''

"Believe it or not, I don't make a practice of
spying on my guests," he said with a growl. She
couldn't hear his footsteps on the dew-damp grass
but she could sense him moving closer.

"Could have fooled me," she assured him cheerfully, remembering how he'd watched her leave on
Jeremy's arm last night. From across the crowded
room she'd felt the impact of his disapproving gaze.

That thought caused her to flick open her long
auburn lashes and she found him standing beside
her. Then she absorbed the running shoes, shorts,
and bare, bronzed torso. Lacey smiled sweetly.
"And anyone who goes jogging at this hour of the
morning certainly has no right to make remarks
about my personal habits."

"I run, Miss Seldon; I do not jog," he informed
her with the typical disdain of the one type of en-
thusiast for the other. He crouched down beside her
and grinned. "Care to join me? The path starts right
over there...." He waved vaguely to indicate a
point behind a clump of trees. "Which accounts for
my presence near your cottage."

"I see. Thank you for the invitation," Lacey said

politely, eyes sparkling in amusement. "But as you have noticed, I have my own program for getting the day started."

"So I gather," he admitted, his glance going to the casually knotted coil of hair which had been clipped to the back of her head. Wispy tendrils trailed down the back of her neck above the low, round collar of her embroidered peasant blouse. Something in his look made her aware of the fact that she wasn't wearing a bra. "But don't you like the idea of beginning your days the same way you end them? With a certain *togetherness?*"

"An intriguing thought," she mused, knowing he was referring to her departure the previous evening. "Perhaps I should run over and wake up Jeremy."

"Come now," he chided firmly. "Let's be sensible about this. Jeremy is undoubtedly sleeping quite soundly. I, on the other hand, am here, I'm awake, and I'm willing...."

"You're also becoming rather aggressive. Perhaps you ought to get on with your run and work some of that excess energy out of your system."

His mouth twisted wryly. "Give me a chance, Lacey. I'm trying to apologize."

"Apologize!" She stared at him.

"I realized after you left last night that I had been behaving in a totally uncalled for manner," he told her with sudden seriousness. "I'm surprised you even bothered to stay on here. I was half expecting you to come to the office this morning and tell me you'd decided to go elsewhere for the summer!''

She hesitated for a split second, wishing she wasn't quite so conscious of the lean power in his smoothly muscled body. But in the morning sunlight there was something elementally attractive about the sweep of broad chest, the strength of hair-roughened thighs, and the curve of shoulder and arm. The very maleness of him seemed to tug at her senses in a way which was disquieting. In spite of herself she recalled the feel of his arms around her on the dance floor. Firmly she thrust that thought aside.

''You're...uh...worried about losing the business?'' she taunted lightly.

He grimaced. ''It would serve me right, wouldn't it? All I can say is, I'm sorry for coming on like...like...''

''Like my brother? Or my father? Or any one of a number of other people I left behind in Iowa?'' she suggested helpfully.

''That bad?''

''Don't worry about it,'' she soothed. ''I'm rather used to it. The only difference is that out here, I don't have to pay any attention to it!''

He shot her a quick, probing glance and then smiled crookedly. ''I can see where you might be a little sick of other people always knowing what's best for you."

"It's not that they know what's best for me," she corrected carefully, thoughtfully. "It's that they know what's *proper* for me. There's a difference. When I was younger I let myself be forced into the mold because I really did think the two were synonymous. The right thing to do, was also the best for me. I've finally realized that's not true. People want you to do the *right* thing because it makes life more comfortable for *them!* Not because it's necessarily the best thing for you!"

"And finally, at the age of twenty-nine, you've realized that, hmmm?"

"I've simply realized that I've missed one hell of a lot in life by conforming to the mold established for me. I want out. It's as straightforward as that." She shrugged.

"And the first thing you run into when you hit the Promised Land is someone else who tries to clamp the lid back on." He groaned self-deprecatingly. "All I can say is, I'm sorry and there were extenuating circumstances."

Lacey bit her lip and then grinned spontaneously. "If you want to know the truth, I didn't really mind listening to your lectures."

"You didn't!" He looked genuinely astonished.

"No. You see, back home I had to listen to that sort of thing and conform, or risk humiliating my whole family and scandalizing the community. Out here I can laugh at such lectures and go off and do exactly as I please. It was rather exhilarating being able to tell you to go to hell last night. Sort of symbolic, if you know what I mean.''

Holt ran a disgusted hand through the thickness of his hair and shook his head. ''I understand,'' he rasped, ''but for the record, I don't like the idea of playing that particular role.''

''But you do it so well!'' she protested on a gurgle of laughter.

''As I said, there were extenuating circumstances,'' he retorted heavily. Instinct told her he was seeking some sort of comprehension and forgiveness.

''I know,'' she said, voice softening. ''You told me. You had a preconception of me before I arrived and you felt obligated to protect that poor, sheltered creature from Jeremy. On top of that, I appeared to be making the same sort of struggle to escape that you once made. I can see where you got caught up with the notion that you had to warn me.''

The silvery eyes narrowed glittering in the bright sunlight. ''That, Lacey Seldon, is only part of it,'' he stated meaningfully.

She blinked. ''What's the rest?''

''I took one look at you yesterday when you arrived and told myself I wanted to get to know you better. And the first thing that happened was Jeremy

Todd. I hoped you'd show up alone last night. I planned to commandeer you for the evening and instead, Todd got the honors. I'm afraid most of those warnings, true as they were, were issued out of sheer masculine resentment of another man's swifter maneuvering!''

"Oh!"

"Don't look so astonished! I know you've classified me as one of the crowd you're busy putting behind you, but that doesn't mean I'm not capable of being attracted to you!''

She lifted her chin inquiringly. "Are you?" She waited a little breathlessly for his response. His admission threw a whole new light on the situation. Or did it? He hadn't exactly denied that the original reasons for his behavior still obtained. He'd just told her they were only part of the motivation behind his actions.

"Is that so hard to believe? You're a rather intriguing woman, Lacey Seldon. Will you let me apologize for my behavior last night?''

"How?"

"Have breakfast with me on my boat this morning. I'll have the kitchen prepare something and we can leave in about an hour. I'll show you some of the island from the water angle," he urged.

Lacey considered the invitation. "Well, I suppose I do have all summer to answer my job-inquiry responses," she agreed, slowly, smiling. "All right.

I'll have breakfast with you. Besides, it's not just a sailboat I've never been on. I've never been on anything except a rowboat!''

The expression in his eyes lightened. ''At least I'll be able to do something that won't remind you of what you're leaving behind! Wear some soft-soled shoes. I'll see you in an hour down by the dock in front of the inn.''

She nodded as he straightened, watching as he set off for the path in an easy, loping run. Then Lacey got to her feet, dusted off the back of her snug-fitting jeans, and headed for the cottage with a sense of anticipation. Life was definitely looking up nicely. Two different men in as many days. Who would have believed it of her?

And they certainly were different, she told herself, pouring a cup of coffee in the sunny little kitchen and taking a seat at the small table by the window. Jeremy Todd was almost exactly what she had been expecting. He had proved pleasant company and she thought their fundamental approach to life was quite similar.

She had let him kiss her when he'd taken her back to the cottage the previous evening, although she hadn't invited him inside. It had been a pleasant enough experience, although not the exciting sensation she had subconsciously been hoping to find. But, then, just because a man might be more interesting and more compatible in some respects than the sort she'd left back in Iowa, that didn't necessarily mean his kisses would be all that different.

Now there was the prospect of a morning to be spent on a boat with a man she could at least amuse herself with by teasing when he grew too pompous. She wondered if Holt Randolph would try to kiss her, too. Poor man. What would he do if she initiated the kiss?

The speculation provided a certain inner laughter which was still in her eyes an hour later when Lacey made her way down to the boat dock in front of the inn. A handsome cabin cruiser gleamed whitely in the sun, and on its deck she saw Holt moving about, dressed now in a pair of faded jeans. The smooth muscles of his back moved easily, almost sensually to her eyes.

He came forward as she walked along the short dock, a definite wariness in his politely welcoming expression. For an instant Lacey wondered at that and then put it aside.

"Breakfast ready?" she called cheerfully.

"And waiting," he replied, assisting her into the gently rocking boat. She glanced around with interest, sensing his pride in the sleek craft.

"Let's hope I'm not the seasick type."

"If you are, you can count on being hung over the side by your heels. I'm not having my deck ruined!" he shot back humorously.

"Not even by a paying customer?"

"I don't take paying customers out on *Reality*," he informed her with a touch of arrogance as he loosened the ropes that bound them to the dock.

"Only friends?"

"Good friends," he emphasized, coiling the ropes and coming forward to start the engine.

She smiled. "As a *friend*, do I have the privilege of asking you where you got the name *Reality?*" Lacey took the seat he indicated as the engine hummed to life and the boat began moving slowly away from the side.

He flicked her a speculative glance. "Are you sure you want to know? It's liable to reopen a conversation you closed rather forcibly last night."

Suddenly she understood. "The name of the boat is a reference to what you supposedly learned at the time you tried your big escape?" Her voice was almost gentle as she asked the question. After all, it couldn't be very pleasant for him to remember that failed effort.

The funny part was, she couldn't really see Holt Randolph failing at whatever he put his mind to. Had there been other factors at work which had made it impossible for him to find another life-style than the one obviously ordained for him by his family? The mystery ex-fiancée?

"Something like that," he agreed cautiously, his attention focused on guiding the boat out of the small bay. "Do you want to hear about it?"

"I don't know," she tossed back saucily, eyes wicked as she lifted her face sunward. "Will I find it depressing?"

"Probably." He sighed. "I guess we'd better skip it for now. I'm glad to see you brought a hat," he added, noting the bright yellow straw object she had remembered at the last minute. "It can get warm out here."

"Have you lived on this island all your life?" she asked interestedly, turning to gaze at the heavily wooded shoreline.

"I spent my summers here while I was growing up. My folks lived in Tacoma and my father's parents ran the inn. I think my grandfather had visions of my father taking over the place eventually but dad had already built a career for himself in engineering by the time that became a genuine possibility."

"You, on the other hand, were an ideal substitute, right?" Lacey chuckled knowingly.

He lifted one shoulder negligently. "It's a long story."

"Well, I suppose what counts is whether or not you're happy now," Lacey said quietly, not looking at him. "Are you glad you made the choice to do what the family wanted and take over the inn?"

"You mean, am I glad I faced reality?" he returned evenly.

"Is that what it amounted to?" She swung her head around to meet his direct look.

"Yes."

"And are you happy?" The laughter was gone from her face as she waited with a deep sense of curiosity for his answer.

"I'm satisfied with my choice." The words came coolly, accompanied by a deliberate nod. His light brown hair caught the sunlight reflecting off the water and Lacey's eyes found a certain pleasure in the sight. She was unaware of how the deep red-brown of her own simply styled hair was doing much the same thing. The light reflecting on it caught the deeply buried fire there. A fire which was somewhat extinguished when she remembered to put on the yellow straw hat.

"If you're satisfied, that's the important thing," she informed him condescendingly.

"But you weren't satisfied back in Iowa?"

"Far from it." She glanced up at him from beneath the yellow brim. "And that's enough of that conversations. As you said, it's one we closed out last night. Where are we going now?"

He paused as if debating whether or not to push the first subject; then he said in an easy tone, "There's a pleasant little cove on the tip of the island. I thought we'd anchor in it and have breakfast on board the boat. Sound okay?"

"Sounds great. I'm not sick yet, you'll notice," she pointed out cheerily.

"I should hope not! This water is as calm as a swimming pool today!" A sudden thought brought his head sharply around. "Good lord! I never thought to ask. You do know how to swim, don't you?"

"Of course! We may not have oceans back in Iowa but we do have rivers and pools!"

"That's a relief. One tends to take swimming for granted out here."

"Afraid I'll fall overboard?" she teased.

"Or get pushed. One never knows," he agreed smoothly.

"Don't worry, as long as you're going to feed me a good breakfast, I won't do anything which might tempt you to push me into Puget Sound!"

"I'll keep that in mind."

The banter set the seal on the truce Holt Randolph seemed intent on declaring. Lacey relaxed, enjoying herself in a glow of satisfaction. She couldn't remember a morning as pleasant as this one ever dawning back in Iowa. She had made the right move there was no doubt about it.

Her inner mood must have been clearly reflected in her smiling face as Holt dropped anchor in a sheltered cove near the isolated southern tip of the island. He grinned at her as he secured the boat and prepared to duck into the cabin for the picnic basket.

"You look like a little cat sunning herself after swallowing a fat canary," he accused lightly, reappearing a moment later.

"That's what I feel like." She stretched in the warmth and leaned back against the cushion of her seat. "Except that I'm still waiting for the canary. Got a nice plump one in that basket?"

"I'm not sure about canaries but we do seem to have a few croissants, strawberries, smoked salmon, and—" he rummaged a bit further in the basket he'd retrieved from the cabin "—orange juice. Will that do?" He looked up expectantly.

"Perfectly."

They consumed the delicacies in the basket with civilized greed and afterward Holt made coffee in the tiny galley of the boat. The conversation flowed freely between them, each careful not to bring up the one topic which threatened discord.

"Maybe I'm a born sailor," Lacey suggested, sipping her coffee contentedly. "I feel great!"

"In that case we'll have to go island hopping one of these days," Holt told her, his eyes meeting hers over the rim of his cup. "The San Juan Islands are strung out all the way to Canada. Would you like that?"

Lacey was about to reply with eager agreement when a small tinge of caution rushed across her mind. Holt was seeking to move their relationship rather quickly along the new lines he'd established. Only last night he'd been lecturing sternly. He was still the same man, she reminded herself deliberately. He'd admitted he was attracted to her, found her interesting, but she knew he hadn't experienced any abrupt change of thinking in the past twenty-four hours. He still disapproved of her intentions.

"We'll see," she demurred politely, busying herself with repacking the remains of the shipboard picnic. She was aware of him watching her silently, as if turning her nonanswer over in his mind. "Please thank your kitchen staff for me. That's the best breakfast I've ever had! Or maybe it's just that everything is going to taste better out here than it did back in Iowa!" she concluded happily.

She went suddenly still as Holt put out a hand and tipped up her chin. The humor of a few moments ago had vanished, leaving his strongly carved face intent and serious.

"Let's find out, shall we?" he murmured, leaning forward.

"Find out what?" she whispered, a strange sensation alerting her nerve endings. He was going to kiss her and she was startled at her uncertainty.

"Find out if everything is going to taste better out here...."

He lowered his head, the hand under her chin sliding around the nape of her neck beneath the darkness of her hair. He kissed her in the shadow of her hat brim, his mouth finding hers with a bold, exploratory manner.

Lacey waited, letting herself experience the probing kiss while she decided how to deal with it. Last night when Jeremy had taken her briefly in his arms, she had been primarily aware of a very pleasant anticipation. An anticipation which, as it turned out, had been quite unfulfilled. But she was practical enough not to feel any great disappointment over that. Jeremy was, after all, only the beginning....

But there was something different operating here she realized as Holt's mouth began to move warmly, questioningly on hers. It was a factor which had been missing last night. A factor, said her slowly activating sense of sensual awareness, which had been missing in Harold's prosaic kisses and in the almost casual embraces she had known with her ex-husband.

A factor which, abruptly and quite unexpectedly, threatened to take away her breath.

The realization shocked her even as Holt moved to deepen the kiss.

"Lacey?"

Her name was a husky question against her lips but he wasn't waiting for an answer, at least not a verbal one. The strong, slightly callus-roughened fingers at the back of her neck tightened perceptibly as if Holt suddenly feared she would try to flee before the growing onslaught he was launching against her senses.

Lacey did attempt to recoil as he coaxed apart her lips, questing between them with the tip of his demanding tongue. Her small movement of withdrawal wasn't made because the masculine assault frightened her, but because it was growing into something she sensed she might not be able to control. And she'd never been faced with quite that sort of situation. It made her wary.

But when she put a hand on his shoulder, tentatively pushing to put some distance between them, Holt groaned a soft protest deep into her throat and his other arm wrapped firmly around her waist, holding her yet closer.

Then, with a swift movement of easy strength he lifted her onto his lap.

"Holt!" she tried vainly, her voice a broken thread of sound as her breathing quickened, "I don't think we should..."

He stopped her faltering words, his mouth closing aggressively over hers once again. She was cradled against his thighs, her head thrown back onto his shoulder where her hair fanned across his bare skin. She was violently aware of the sun-heated warmth of his chest and the muscles of his legs. The position made her feel dismayingly vulnerable.

"Don't say anything, Lacey," he rasped against

her cheek. "No words. Not yet. Some things are better understood without words...."

He buried his mouth in the curve of her throat and his hand slid along her denim-covered hip, up under the flowing peasant blouse to the contour of her stomach.

Lacey shivered at the touch and a small sigh escaped her. She told herself she ought to take the situation in hand, if she still could, but the gentle rocking of the boat seemed to be adding a hypnotic effect to the captivating sensations of his lips and hands. Instead of trying again to pull away, she lifted her fingertips to the thickness of his hair, reveling in it.

"Oh, Holt..."

Her words seemed to release yet another bond in both of them. The warm, strong hand on her stomach flattened possessively against her skin and began gliding upward toward her unconfined breasts.

Too late Lacey realized his intention. What was the matter with her? She barely knew this man and wasn't even sure she liked the part she did know! What was she doing allowing him to hold her and kiss her like this?

With an extraordinary effort of will she twisted in his grasp, intending to slide off his lap. But the arm cradling her to his chest suddenly became a band of steel clamping her in place while his fingers moved to shape the small, high breasts.

"Lacey, don't fight me. I only want to sample some of your sweetness. You feel so good. I wanted to kiss you the moment I saw you yesterday.... Hell, I wanted to do a lot more than that! I took one look at the excitement and anticipation in those lovely blue eyes and I wanted you to be feeling those emotions for *me!*"

"Holt, please! This has gone far enough.... I hardly know you and..."

"No," he denied deeply, his tongue circling the delicate area of her ear. "You don't have to worry about how far you go with a stranger as long as the feelings are right. You told me so yourself!"

"I meant..."

Her protest died beneath the sharply indrawn breath which she found herself gulping as his thumb grated lightly, excitingly across one nipple, enticing it to urgent firmness.

"The feelings are right, aren't they, Lacey?" he challenged softly as he felt her shiver again in his arms. His fingers shifted, circling the other nipple and bringing it to a thrusting peak.

Lacey moaned into his shoulder, felt the damp film on his hot skin and inhaled the intoxicating scent of him. Without conscious thought she sank her small, white teeth into his shoulders. He growled a fierce response and the hand on her breast moved with an exciting tension.

Her nails dug into his back as he lifted the blouse

upward and lowered his head to find the tip of one breast.

"Oh!"

The small cry was torn from her as her senses spun. Never had her body reacted so positively, so immediately to a man's touch! She knew intuitively that this fire that raced along her nerves and brought one tremor after another must be the element of passion she had told herself existed but which she had never really known, not even during the year and a half of her marriage.

"Lacey, Lacey," he rasped, his tongue flicking narrowing circles around the dark pink which crowned her breast, closing in on the nipple with tantalizing, teasing slowness until she thrust her fingers heavily into his hair and forced his mouth more tightly against her.

With a groan of male satisfaction and rising need, he obliged, kissing her until she was a tightly coiled human spring searching for the ultimate release.

With a powerful surge he was suddenly on his feet, lifting her high against his chest and carrying her toward the small cabin. She shut her eyes against the brightness of the sun and the full impact of what she knew was happening. A moment later she was lowered gently to the cushion of a narrow bed and when her lashes fluttered open he was coming down on top of her. His solid, lean weight pinned her to the bunk.

Gripping her tightly, his lower body pressing deliberately, intimately against her, Holt rained kisses along her throat, down her breasts, and across the softness of her stomach. The blouse was off completely now. He'd pulled it swiftly, impatiently over her head and flung it to one side.

"My God! I want you so badly," he grated hoarsely. "I can't ever remember wanting a woman this suddenly, this badly before in my life! I feel as though I'd been drugged!"

She heard the near-violent need and passion in him and responded to it, her arms going around his neck as she turned her lips into his throat and then found the sensitive earlobe with her teeth.

Lacey knew she was lost to everything now but the feel of this man who had so swiftly, so completely set her senses aflame. He made her keenly aware of his desire, his hardness pressing into her, begging to be enveloped by her softness, and she could no longer think of denying him or herself.

His hands were on the snap of her jeans, tugging it free and then sliding inside the loosened waistband. She heard his sharp breath as he caressed her with increasing intimacy, seeking to know her fully.

"I'm going to learn every inch of you, make you mine completely," he vowed huskily. He felt her tremble beneath him and gave a deep, exultant laugh. "Is this what you came so far to find, my sweet little librarian? Is this what was missing back in Iowa?''

"Oh, Holt! I never knew it could be like this! I never realized...'' she gasped, her head moving restlessly on the cushion as he first tasted and then gently nibbled at the curve of her stomach.

"I'm glad,'' he whispered forcefully. "I'm glad you're going to find your answers here in my arms. Did you think to find them so quickly?'' he added with a flash of satisfied humor. He began to push the jeans down over the swell of her hips.

"So quickly?'' Lacey repeated, the words somehow forcing a path past the whirl of emotion. "No!''

What was she doing? This was too much, too soon. She wanted to know this passion fully but in spite of her plans for freedom and experiment, she had never intended being swept up into this sort of brief encounter!

"Holt, stop! You must stop! I never meant to let this happen....''

His hands stilled, his fingers digging into her flesh as he lifted his head to stare at her. The silvery eyes were molten with desire, narrowing warily as he absorbed the sudden panic in her face.

"We can't stop now, Lacey. It's too late. You want to find out where all this leads as much as I do! Don't deny it!''

She shuddered. "It's too soon. Too soon! I don't want..."

"You wanted an affair," he interrupted roughly.

"A *love* affair!" she cried wretchedly. "Not a...a meaningless encounter with a man I barely know. A man with whom I have nothing in common."

"Give it a chance, Lacey," he half ordered, half pleaded. "You can't say it's meaningless. Nothing this strong could be without meaning!"

"You don't understand," she wailed, pushing at his shoulders, her fingers outstretched on his skin as she tried to dislodge him.

"Damn it! You can't go this far and then call a halt!"

"Yes, I can! I can do anything I damn well please," she flung back, letting a mounting anger supply the necessary motivation to stop him. "That's why I came out West, remember? To live my own life!"

She saw the flush of frustrated fury high on his cheekbones and could literally feel him reining in his instincts. She knew with sudden clarity that he wanted to crush her back into the bunk, tear off her jeans, and finish what had been started between them.

The next shiver that coursed through her was one of purely feminine fear. What if he didn't cease at her command? She was playing with fire and she knew it. She'd been a fool. But the exquisite sensations he had generated still percolated through her system, and she didn't think she would ever be able to forget them, even if she talked her way out of this.

But in the next moment she knew she had won the battle of wills. Lacey watched his mouth tighten and his eyes harden, sensed the debate going on within him. Then, without a word, he heaved himself to his feet, turned away with a low, savage exclamation, and threw himself out of the cabin.

Lacey felt the engines come to life as she shakily did up the zipper of her jeans and searched for the peasant blouse. A wave of guilt and a grim acknowledgment of her own responsibility for what had happened made her gather her courage and head for the outer deck.

Holt stood tensely, guiding the boat out of the small bay. He didn't even glance at her when she touched his shoulder tentatively with one hand.

"Holt?" Her voice was weak and she had to make an effort to speak above the muted roar of the engines. "Holt, I'm sorry. You have every right to be angry at me. I'm a big girl now, I should never have allowed that to happen."

His head swung around and she could have sworn she heard the snap of his teeth as he fixed her with a brooding, hostile stare.

"You're sorry!"

"Yes! I know it's not much under the circumstances, but it's all I can say! I don't know what got into me. I had no business leading you on like that when I never had any intention of...of going to bed with you. I can only say I never meant the kiss to get out of hand. Please forgive me. You have my word it won't happen again."

She met his gaze, her own beseeching and deeply apologetic.

He was still staring at her but there was more than a hint of outright astonishment now in his expression. "You *are* sorry!" he exclaimed, throttling the engines and turning full around to confront her.

"I take full responsibility for what happened, of course." She nodded ruefully, sensing his ebbing anger. She tried a grim little smile that didn't quite reach her eyes. "I realize that part of my new lifestyle will involve accepting the obligations as well as the privileges of my freedom. I should have made my position clear to you from the beginning."

He was gazing at her steadily, a glimmer of somewhat stunned amusement beginning to dawn in his eyes. "Have you forgotten," he asked very gravely, "that I'm the one who initiated that kiss which got so out of hand?"

"Of course not!"

"Then doesn't it strike you that I'm the one who ought to be making this little speech of apology?"

he drawled, and now she was certain of the wry humor growing in his expression.

Feeling much more confident, Lacey shook her head. "Not in this instance. I can understand how I failed to make my intentions clear. I told you I was interested in an affair and it's not your fault I didn't explain that I meant something a little more enduring than a one-night, or rather, a one-morning stand!"

He fitted one hand to his hip, leaned back against the gunwale, and regarded her with a slow grin. "I'm not sure I like you taking all the responsibility for this. Looking back on things, I prefer the notion that I might possibly have been doing a good job of seducing you!"

Her own sense of humor bubbled forth at the teasing light in his eyes. "Shall we toss a coin to see who gets to shoulder the blame?"

Holt laughed, reaching out a hand to snag her quickly by the neck and hold her still for a short, hard kiss that was over almost as soon as it had begun. "You are turning out to be filled with surprises, Lacey Seldon. Whatever else happens this summer, I think I can predict life won't be dull!"

"It better not be! I've come much too far to find life dull!"

He slanted her a strange, enigmatic glance. "Yes," he agreed. "Much too far."

# *Four*

During the next few days Lacey felt as though she were walking a tightrope. The sensation was not unpleasant. There was an underlying excitement to it which had been wholly unknown to her back in Iowa.

But it also created a sense of unease which she couldn't quite banish or laugh away. It increased her awareness, made her conscious of a man she would normally have ignored.

Holt Randolph wanted her. She saw it in his eyes every morning when he stopped to talk before beginning his run. He had taken to deliberately walking up behind her while she sat cross-legged on the lawn in front of the rising sun. He waited until she sensed his presence and greeted him. Then he'd move, catlike, until he was in front of her, the blue eyes full of the memories of that morning on the boat as they raked her or caressed her. She was never sure which to expect.

He made no move to re-create the intimacy he had precipitated before but he didn't need to, she acknowledged ruefully. She felt it every time he looked at her.

At night, when she visited the inn with Jeremy or by herself, Holt danced with her, his hold possessive. He wanted her to know of his desire, she decided, but he fully intended to restrain himself. With a secret smile she told herself it was probably because his feelings toward her were as ambivalent as hers were toward him. He didn't approve of her goals and she didn't appreciate his poorly concealed disapproval. His lapses into outright criticism were frequent and she reacted to them with teasing laughter.

"What do you think about out here early in the morning?" he asked one day, hunkering down beside her in his running shorts and shoes, his eyes curious and intent.

"What do you think about when you run?" she countered with a smile.

He hesitated. "Nothing in particular. Whatever comes to mind, I suppose. It's more a process of…of my mind floating along with my body. I just absorb the feelings and sensations. I don't try to concentrate." He looked at her sharply to see if she understood.

"That's how it is for me," Lacey said quietly. "I simply sit here and let my mind compose itself for the day."

"Did you start this regimen back in Iowa?" He chuckled.

"Don't be ridiculous! They would have put me away in a padded cell!" But she knew he understood what she got out of her morning period of quiet, just as she sensed what his running meant to him.

On the occasions when she left the lounge with Jeremy late at night, Lacey could feel the brooding, disquieting impact of Holt's stare as he watched them go. She knew without being told that he wanted to yank her away from the younger man and escort her back to the cottage himself. His restraint intrigued her.

Holt's dancing took on increasingly intimate overtones and on two occasions during which he had held her in an almost loverlike embrace, she had sensed the anger in him when she'd freed herself at the conclusion of the music to go back to Jeremy or rejoin whatever group of guests she had been with.

It was Holt who came and found her lazing beside the indoor pool, chatting with new friends and

idly thumbing through a batch of letters from potential employers the day her mother phoned.

"The office just got a call for you, Lacey," he
told her, nodding to the others around her. "I told
George I thought I'd seen you heading this way."

Lacey leaped to her feet, her expression animated. "Did he say where the call was from?"
George Barton, Holt's assistant, was a pleasant man
in his midfifties who had taken an active interest in
Lacey's job hunting. He always had her stack of
mail ready for her every morning.

"Iowa, I'm afraid." He grinned wickedly as her
face fell. "Expecting something more interesting?"

He watched as she flung on a short, jewel-toned
bathing-suit cover-up over her sleek, sapphire-blue
maillot. She waved the letter in her hand at him.

"Hawaii," she stated succinctly, starting for the
bank of house phones at the edge of the pool. Holt
followed more slowly, stopping en route for an
exchange of greetings with several guests.

"What do you mean, Hawaii?" he hissed, reaching her just as she picked up the phone.

She held the formal business letter out to him as
she spoke into the receiver. He frowned, scanning
the page as she greeted her mother.

"Hi, mom! Of course I'm fine. Didn't you get
my letters? Yes, it's lovely out here."

She paused, listening politely to the expected lit-
any from the other end of the line. "No," Lacey

finally said gently. "I'm not coming back to Iowa.
I like it here. You and dad should come out and see
these islands. Green as far as the eye can see. Not
a cornfield in view!"

"Lacey," Martha Seldon said determinedly,
sensing that the end to her daughter's crisis was not
yet in sight, "don't you think this has gone far
enough? It's all well and good to take a vacation..."

"It's not a vacation, mom," Lacey retorted, trying to keep her tone light. "It's quite permanent.
Please try and understand that."

There was a pause and then her mother threw in
the real reason for the call. "Roger," she said very
meaningfully, "is getting a divorce."

"No kidding? Another one?" Lacey took the
news of her ex-husband's impending freedom with
a complete lack of emotion. "How did you hear
about it?"

Holt's head came up, a frown etching the corners
of his mouth and knitting the tawny brows.

"He called us, Lacey," Mrs. Seldon informed
her in a portentous voice. "He asked to speak to
you."

Lacey shook her head in wry disgust. "Why?"
she asked coolly. "He surely didn't think I'd be
hanging around to comfort and console him, did
he?" But knowing Roger, that was probably exactly what he'd thought. He'd been well aware of

how much Lacey's family approved of him and how Lacey always did as her family and everyone else in town expected.

"Now, Lacey, you know he always cared for you...." Martha Seldon began soothingly. She'd always liked the idea of Lacey marrying a doctor.

"Roger Wesley only cared for me as long as he needed a source of funds to pay off his medical-school debts. When are you and dad going to realize that?" Lacey suddenly grew uncomfortably aware of Holt's presence and turned away to speak more privately into the phone. "I could care less that he's getting a divorce and you have my permission to tell him so!"

"Lacey, sometimes a man needs to sow a few wild oats. Roger didn't get the chance to do it before because he was all wrapped up trying to get through medical school. He's probably worked it out of his system by now and realized that it's you he really wanted all along. Men are like that, dear. Sometimes we women have to be a little understanding...."

Lacey grinned in spite of herself. And then the grin turned into outright laughter. "Oh, mom!"

"Lacey! What's so funny? This is your husband we're talking about!"

"My ex-husband and that's how he's going to stay. Ex. If he asks, you can tell him that I'm sowing some wild oats myself. What's more, this crop is going to be permanent! Good-bye, mom. Give my love to dad. I'll talk to you next week.''

Blue-green eyes still dancing with humor, Lacey hung up the phone. She swung around to find Holt watching her with a narrow, assessing look.

"A last appeal to sanity?" he hazarded dryly, still holding her letter.

"I'm afraid they're having trouble accepting the fact that I really have gone crazy for good." She reached for the paper in his hand. Holt gave it to her.

"Sounds like mom was trying to bait the hook," he went on remotely. "Roger, I take it, is your ex-husband?"

"Newly divorced again, it seems. And going out of his way to tell my parents the news. He knows they always approved of him."

"Meaning he might have visions of getting back his nice, understanding, conforming little wife?"

"Who understands him only too well!"

"Do you hate him?" Holt suddenly asked softly, searchingly.

"Nope. I simply don't care about him one way or the other. Total indifference, I'm afraid."

"Good."

Her eyes widened in surprise at the satisfaction in the single word. "Why do you say that?"

"Because it means you really are over him."

"I was over Roger before he filed for divorce.

He did me a favor. The only reason I didn't file first was because I was having trouble gathering the courage to create the necessary scene. I knew the whole town would be watching, you see.''

"And now you're thinking of taking a job in Hawaii and having an affair. Sowing some wild oats. You've come a long way from Iowa, Lacey Seldon," Holt observed with a cool nod. "Speaking of the affair, when do you plan to start?"

Her chin lifted at the sarcasm. "How do you know it hasn't already started?" she asked sweetly, deliberately glancing across the pool to where Jeremy had just entered and was searching for a vacant lounger.

Holt shrugged. "I know."

"Spying on your guests again?" she chided irritably.

"I prefer to think of it as keeping an eye on you," he murmured placatingly.

"Why?" she snapped.

"You know the answer to that. I'll bet even back in Iowa a woman knows when a man is contemplating pursuit!"

"But, Holt," Lacey retorted, fighting back the rush of warmth she was experiencing at his unsubtle words, "you can't be implying that you're interested in me personally. After all, you don't approve of me. And you're much too self-controlled to allow yourself to go crazy over a woman of whom you don't approve!''

Even as she taunted him in self-defense, Lacey felt the surge of excitement of having him finally state his intentions. He was the wrong man. Not at all the sort with whom she would seriously consider beginning an affair. But the sensual electricity which followed between them was undeniable and she knew that even if he wasn't right for her in some ways, he nevertheless had the power to create some of the sensations she had been longing to discover.

''What gives you such faith in my self-control?'' he inquired with a new silkiness in his voice that touched off faint alarms in her.

''You've been a model of restraint since that breakfast on the boat,'' she reminded him kindly. ''I'm sure you're determined not to suffer any further lapses.''

''I wasn't aware you'd even noticed my restraint.''

''Noticed and admired it,'' she assured him, not stopping to consider the potential danger in baiting him like this. The excitement of the tightrope was growing stronger, more alluring. ''You do set a fine example for us more impetuous types. But, then, it wouldn't do to become involved with a woman who was as free-spirited as I am, would it?''

"No," he admitted blandly. "Not unless I found a way to curb the free spirit."

Lacey's eyes slitted. For just an instant she saw something in him which wasn't at all restrained or controlled. It was gone almost immediately but she knew with a small chill that she'd caught a glimpse of a very primitive male intent which lay below the surface of Holt Randolph.

"It can't be done," she said flatly. "As we say back in the Midwest, I've got the bit between my teeth. I'm going to run as far as I can for as long as I please until I find exactly what I want."

"You're so determined to run that there's every possibility you'll race right past your goal without ever seeing it!"

"I doubt it," Lacey countered airily, "but even if that should happen, there are always other goals, other destinations."

"You're bent on sampling them all?"

"As many as I can!" She saw no point in compromising her statement by mentioning that she still retained a portion of her inborn common sense. It sounded much more dramatic this way!

"What if this affair you're looking for turns out to be very long-term?" he suggested coolly. "Won't that tie you down?"

"Affairs, by their very nature, don't tend to last long." She eyed him stonily.

"As soon as you grow bored or restless or as

soon as something more amusing comes along, you'll be on your way, right?''

''There's no sense trying to force an unhappy relationship. Or are you one of those old-fashioned types who believes two people should stay together regardless of how miserable they are?''

''No,'' he denied slowly. ''But I'm pragmatic enough to realize there are going to be some rough times in every relationship, and I wouldn't want to be involved with a woman who was lured away when something brighter appeared on the horizon.''

''Then you certainly don't want to mess about with someone flighty like me,'' she retorted in understanding accents, deliberately trying to goad him.

''You may not be as radical as you think you are. You're the one, after all, who told me she wanted more than a one-night stand,'' he reminded her firmly. ''And look at the evidence. You've been here a whole week and there's still no sign of you and Jeremy Todd beginning a torrid affair. Why is that? Isn't he proving interesting enough to warrant at least a summer fling?''

''That's none of your business!'' Lacey was stung into replying. Damned if she was going to admit to this man that she wasn't finding the excitement she sought with Jeremy; that her relationship with the young would-be writer was in danger of remaining merely a friendly association.

Holt's face softened as he studied the warning signals in Lacey's blue-green eyes. "You're right." He surprised her by agreeing humbly. A little too humbly, perhaps, she decided cautiously. "But if it's true that you haven't made any sort of commitment to Todd, you're free to have dinner with me tonight, aren't you?"

"Am I expected to leap at the opportunity of sitting across the table from you and listening to your cautionary tales all evening?" she managed crisply, taken aback by the unexpected invitation.

But even as she chided him, Lacey knew she was going to accept. There was so much she wanted to know about Holt Randolph, not the least of which was how far this restraint of his went. It was pure female curiosity driving her, she decided, and such curiosity could be a dangerous goad, but she couldn't deny the impulse to satisfy it.

"I promise I won't lecture." Holt's smile was sudden and beguiling. "If you'll accept the invitation, I'll give you my word I won't say a single disapproving word about sowing wild oats."

Lacey hesitated before tipping her head quizzically to one side with a mocking expression.

"Word of honor?"

"Word of honor," he repeated solemnly.

She nodded. "All right. I have a feeling the evening's going to be hard on you, though. How will you resist the temptation to try and set my feet back on the straight and narrow?''

''As you've observed, I can be a model of restraint under certain circumstances. Just think how much fun you'll have teasing and tormenting me all evening!''

''You could be right.'' She grinned. ''What time shall I come up to the lodge?''

Holt shook his head. ''I'll pick you up. We're not eating here tonight; I feel like taking the evening off. George can handle the brandy hour. There's a great place for salmon in the village. Six-thirty okay?''

''I'm learning to love salmon,'' Lacey told him with genuine enthusiasm, as she thought of the Northwest specialty. ''I'll be ready.''

She felt his eyes on her as she gravely excused herself and went off to show Jeremy the inquiry letter from the engineering firm in Hawaii which needed a documentation manager. Jeremy, at least, would be happy for her.

But Lacey couldn't resist talking about it at dinner, either.

''Naturally there's nothing settled yet. The letter I got today was only an expression of interest,'' she found herself telling Holt several hours later as they sat by a window overlooking the island's quiet harbor.

The restaurant was one of those casual waterfront

places with a kitchen that contrived to turn out truly elegant fish. Holt and his date had been greeted warmly by the friendly management and shown to the best table in the house. It paid to go out with someone who had contacts in the restaurant business, Lacey had decided when a complimentary bottle of wine had been sent to the table.

"Hasn't there been anything else of interest in those stacks of mail George gets for you every morning?" Holt demanded, watching her dig into her appetizer of steamed clams.

"A couple of possibilities in California. One with an architectural-engineering firm and one with a small college in Los Angeles. Most of the rest of the mail has been the usual form letter thanking me for my application and promising to consider me for any opening which occurs. But that Hawaii job could be something really special. What an opportunity! Imagine living in the islands for a year or two!"

"You're already living on an island," he noted wryly.

"It's hardly the same thing!" she protested, thinking of balmy Hawaiian nights. On Holt's island one often had to build a fire in the evening to take off the chill!

"What will you do if that position doesn't come through? What if nothing very interesting comes through by fall?"

"Worried you're going to still have me hanging around all winter?" She chuckled.

"Is that a distinct possibility?" he murmured.

Lacey laughed outright. "Don't worry. I've got a couple of other ideas tucked away."

He looked fascinated, watching her animated face with great attention. "Like what?"

"You're really interested?" She lifted one eyebrow rather skeptically.

"I've already told you that you intrigue me." He growled softly, the intent gleam in his eyes darkening.

"This is something I've never discussed with anyone," Lacey began slowly, wondering what was prompting her to do so now.

"I'm listening," he encouraged, reaching for a chunk of sourdough bread and liberally spreading it with butter.

"Well, I'm thinking of going into business for myself. Perhaps doing some consulting. All sorts of companies need advise on setting up and maintaining files, establishing microfilming programs for their records, things like that. Or perhaps I'll try something totally new like being a travel agent or running a boutique...."

"You're really searching, aren't you?" Holt asked gently, with an unexpected degree of genuine understanding in his deep tones. He hesitated and then said quietly, "I went searching once...."

"I know and it didn't work. You promised we wouldn't discuss that topic," Lacey interrupted softly.

"I promised not to lecture. I was merely going to tell you a little about myself. Aren't you interested?" He looked hurt.

Guilt overwhelmed her as she realized she was making a habit of steering him away from any personal conversation about himself. Impulsively she stretched a hand across the table and touched his. "Yes." She smiled warmly, honestly. "I want to know something about you. The only reason I shy away from the subject is because I'm afraid you're only using it as a wedge to give me more sound advice."

His fingers closed around her own and he answered her smile with an intimate, knowing look. "I gave you my word earlier. I'll keep it. No lectures."

"So tell me about your brief, wild flight to freedom," she challenged, laughingly removing her hand as the salmon arrived.

"Where shall I begin? I've told you it's a long story. I practically grew up at the inn. My parents traveled a lot due to my dad's job. He was always going to odd places around the world. My grandparents often took me to stay on the island and somewhere along the line everyone just started assuming that one day I'd take over the inn."

"Did your parents encourage that notion, too?"

"Oh, yes. My grandfather was a very aggressive, single-minded man. He wanted the inn to stay in the family and he'd resigned himself to the fact that my father wasn't going to take over the place. That left me. Mom and dad were happy enough to get him off their backs and have him turn his attention to me as the future heir!"

"How did you feel about it?" Lacey asked keenly, empathizing with a little boy who found himself being groomed and directed from his earliest years toward a specific goal.

"I didn't fight it. I loved the place as a kid and worked here summers while I was in school. By the time I graduated from college it seemed logical to take over running the inn full-time. But there was a hitch. It turned out that my grandfather, in spite of his claims, wasn't about to retire. It just didn't work having two stubborn Randolphs trying to manage the place."

"I'll bet!" Lacey could imagine Holt's determination and will matched against an older version of himself. The irresistible force and the immovable object.

Holt lifted one shoulder in silent agreement, his expression wry. "To shorten the tale, as you might have guessed, granddad and I quarreled more and more frequently. I finally told him I was going to find something else to do with my life and walked out.''

''What happened?'' Lacey was enthralled.

''The family yelled blue murder, naturally. They all claimed I was walking away from my responsibilities, that my grandparents had been led to *count* on me.''

''I can hear it now!'' Lacey nodded her head understandingly.

''I told them to forget their plans for me, that I was formulating my own. And I did,'' he concluded simply, reaching for his wineglass.

''You really left it all behind?'' Lacey couldn't keep the skepticism out of her voice.

''Umm-hmmm. Got a job with an international hotel firm and wound up managing the start-up of hotels all over the world. It was an interesting life. I got to live in Acapulco, the Bahamas, Europe, and Asia.''

Lacey sighed enviously. ''It sounds marvelous.''

The edge of his mouth quirked. ''It was. Fast, exciting… Everything you're looking for, in fact.''

''Everything?''

''Yes,'' he assured her blandly, ''including the affairs.''

''Holt!''

''You're turning pinker than the salmon on your plate,'' he noted in amusement.

''Never mind that,'' she gritted, mentally pushing

aside the thought of Holt involved in a series of torrid love affairs. It was too disturbing. "Tell me what happened next. How did you wind up back here?"

"I think I'll tell you Chapter Two of my life story some other time," he said with abrupt decisiveness, pouring her another glass of the crisp Washington State Chenin Blanc.

"I want to hear it now," she protested eagerly, ignoring his actions.

"One of the things I've learned in life is that we don't always get what we want precisely when we want it," he teased, eyes glinting. "Eat your fish before it gets cold."

"You're doing this to annoy me, aren't you?" She groaned ruefully. "You know I won't rest until I hear the rest of the tale!"

"Excellent," he murmured in tones of utmost satisfaction. "It will give you something to think about tonight after I take you back to the cottage."

"You want me to think about you?" she dared, glancing up at him through lowered lashes.

"That's exactly what I want," he tossed back imperturbably, picking up his fork and paying no attention to the obvious flirtation.

## Five

Once Lacey gave up the futile attempt to coax Holt into giving her the rest of the story, the conversation moved easily between them again, as easily as it always did when they weren't clashing over the issue of her future.

She was turning that realization over in her mind when Holt brought his silver Alfa Romeo sports car to a halt in his private parking space at the inn.

"Going to invite me inside?" he demanded softly as he walked her up the path to her cottage.

Lacey slanted him a calculating glance, wondering if she would. It was a question she had been asking herself off and on for an hour.

"If I do, will you tell me the second half of your story?" she tried.

"Not a chance. I'm going to get all the mileage I can out of it and that means keeping you dangling."

They were at the door of the cottage and Holt calmly took the key from Lacey's hand and inserted it. He was in the room, nonchalantly beginning to build a fire before she realized she hadn't actually invited him.

With a tiny, wry smile Lacey went into the kitchen and made a pot of tea. Holt appeared to be intending to stay awhile.

She emerged a few minutes later to the sensual strains of a flamenco guitar.

"Found my record collection, I see." She smiled, seating herself and pouring the Darjeeling tea.

"Your taste in music is as reckless as the rest of you," Holt drawled, sitting down beside her and reaching for the cup and saucer. "But who am I to complain?"

"Understanding as you do the crisis I'm going through?" she concluded for him tauntingly. The full skirt of her soft, ruffled summer dress spread across the sofa cushion as Lacey slipped off her sandals and tucked one ankle under her.

He shrugged, the silvery eyes meeting hers over the rim of the cup. "Would you laugh in my face if I told you that what you're looking for isn't going to be what you really want? That when you find it, you're going to be disappointed?"

"Yes, I'd laugh. And we agreed not to discuss the issue."

"During dinner. But dinner is over now."

He set down his cup, the firm line of his mouth hardening slightly as he studied her for a long moment. "I don't think I want to listen to any more of your laughter tonight," he finally grated in a husky whisper that roused her nerves into starting awareness.

Lacey smiled coolly. She was alert to the new and perhaps dangerous element in the atmosphere, but for the life of her she couldn't resist goading him just a little further. Why was she so eager to push him like this?

"I'm turning into a regular source of amusement for you, aren't I?" he muttered reflectively.

"Isn't it your avowed aim to keep the customers happy?" she quipped.

He reached out and deliberately removed the cup from her hand, setting it down beside his.

"Anything for the customers," he agreed thickly, pulling her into his arms.

Lacey didn't resist. A part of her knew that letting Holt Randolph kiss her probably wasn't the smartest thing she could do going at the moment, but hadn't she recently abandoned a life of doing only the "smart thing"?

She felt his hand tangle in the thickness of her

hair as he bore her back into the cushions until she was pinned beneath his weight.

"For a week I've been lying awake at night thinking about what happened on my boat," he said, growling. His mouth moved tantalizingly across hers, teasing apart her lips until she moaned gently.

His tongue invaded with exciting abruptness, mastering the sweet territory of her mouth with an urgency which echoed through the length of his body. Lacey felt herself respond to the hardening demand in him and her fingers clenched involuntarily into the muscles of his shoulders as the kiss deepened.

"I've been going crazy dancing with you every evening, seeing you each morning and not letting myself hold you like this...."

"Such restraint," she taunted invitingly, closing her eyes as he began to trace the line of her cheekbones with his lips, seeking her ear.

"I needed time to think," he said heavily.

She raked her fingers lightly down his back, across the material of his shirt and felt him arch against her in response. "And have you done all your thinking?" she murmured.

"Most of it," he affirmed and then cut off her next words with a sharp nip at her ear. It was an effective ploy. Lacey drew in her breath and felt herself melt beneath the onslaught.

Her senses began to swirl around her as they had that morning on the boat, tuning out the rest of the world and concentrating only on the man who had stirred them to life.

She twisted beneath him as he swept his hand down her side, his thumb gliding briefly, thrillingly across the nipple of one breast before going on to shape her hip.

Lacey moaned again and heard his answering murmur of desire.

"Lacey, Lacey, tell me you need me," he commanded roughly, his fingers digging into the softness of her derriere. His lips buried themselves in her throat. "Give me that much, at least!"

"Holt, I..." Her words were broken off as her body responded with steadily rising passion to his touch. "I don't understand how you can do this to me!" she finally got out with stark honesty, clinging to him.

He emitted a deep, satisfied crack of laughter, using his teeth lightly on the skin of her shoulder as he pushed aside the edge of her dress. His legs slid with warm aggression between hers, making her reel with a deliciously ravished feeing even though they were both still clothed. "I've been asking myself the same question for a week from the opposite point of view!" he confessed grimly. "How dare you show up on my island and turn everything upside down?"

"Have I really done that?" she asked wonderingly, glancing up at him through lashes heavy with sensuality as he raised his head to stare down at her.

"You've led a sheltered life indeed if you aren't aware of your own power," he told her a little savagely, lowering his head once more to tease and torment her mouth. With every light, taunting, exciting kiss, his fingers undid another button down the front of her dress.

"Oh!" The soft, feminine cry came as he freed the last of the buttons and then found her thrusting peaks with an insistent, exploring touch.

"I love the feel of you," he whispered gratingly, stringing kisses down her throat and over the swell of her small breasts. "Small and soft and strong. You bring out more than just desire in me, honey. You make me want to possess you completely, body and soul!"

All the warnings which had served to bring her back to reality on the boat floated briefly back into Lacey's mind at his words. She had gone far enough tonight. This man could be dangerous and she wasn't at all certain she was ready to deal with his brand of danger.

She tried to shift her legs gently, move them together once more, and break the intimate contact of their lower bodies. Her hands worked on his shoulders as she tried to short-circuit the electrical charge flowing between them.

"Holt...Holt I think we'd better stop...."

But her voice was horribly weak, even to her own ears and when he closed her mouth with his fingers, ignoring her soft plea, Lacey found herself swallowing the remainder of the protest.

He didn't bother to acknowledge her futile, half-hearted efforts, recognizing them for what they were, she decided vaguely. The actions of a woman caught up between the crush of her own desire and common sense. He was deciding which of the motivations would win out, ordering the outcome of the decision with the masculine power he was learning he exerted over her. "You want me, Lacey. I know you want me," he rasped, sliding the dress off her shoulders, down to her waist. He touched her lingeringly, sensually, intimately. "Say it, I need to hear you say it!"

He kissed the skin of her stomach, sliding down the length of her body before raising himself just long enough to pull the dress over her hips and off completely.

When his body came back down on hers, Lacey was shivering with the force of the desire he had generated. He knew every telltale shudder which went through her. She was fiercely aware of the satisfaction he was taking in her response.

"Tell me, Lacey," he repeated urgently, his

kisses hot and passionate against the skin of her bare stomach. His hands crushed her thighs and then he started probing just inside the elastic band of her satiny brief.

She could deny him no longer. Lacey gave herself up to the spell he had created. Wasn't this what she had been seeking? "I want you, Holt! Oh, my God! How I want you!"

"Show me, sweetheart," he commanded softly. "Please, show me!"

She found the buttons of his shirt, almost unable to unfasten them because her hands were trembling so much. He let her remove the garment and then crushed her once again back into the cushions, appearing to revel in the feel of her tip-hardened breasts against his chest.

The rough, curling hair of his chest teased her nipples until Lacey didn't think she could stand the combination of sensations much longer. Her ankles wrapped around his as she sought to force the hard maleness of him still closer, and the half-blocked sounds in the back of her throat were a soft, seductive plea.

"Please, Holt, please..."

"I've wanted to hear you beg for me ever since you walked into the lobby that first day," he muttered, running a questing, exploring, possessive touch from her taut, full breasts down to the soft mound below her stomach. "Do you know what it

does to me to hear you plead like that? To feel you
writhe beneath me, unable to hide your need?''

"How does it make you feel?'' she challenged
boldly. The seething, passionate rhythms of the flamenco guitar seemed to guide her fingers as she
sought the muscular curve of his buttocks. She glo-
ried in the shuddering response of his body.

"As though I were capturing a free-spirited butterfly and teaching her at last what it means to need
just one man....''

She shivered again at the determination in his
words but she was past caring about anything but
the present. Without protest, she arched her hips
against him, coiling her arms more and more tightly
around his body. Her head fell back in an agony of
exquisite need and she heard his indrawn breath at
the obvious surrender.

And then, with no warning, Holt was breaking
the powerful contact, pulling away reluctantly but
firmly as if he'd reached a preordained stopping
point. As first Lacey didn't realize what was happening.

"Enough, butterfly,'' he whispered, stroking her
soothingly. "Enough.''

"Holt?'' Eyelids heavy with dreamy passion, Lacey looked up at him in the flickering firelight.

His mouth curved with gentleness as he sat up
beside her and bent down to retrieve her dress.
"I'm practicing a little of that restraint you were

admiring earlier,'' he explained quietly, handing the garment to her. His eyes strayed to her breasts and then lifted back firmly to meet her questioning, uncomprehending gaze.

"You're leaving? Just like that?"

Lacey could only stare at him, clutching the fabric of her dress. She didn't want him to leave. Not now. Not when he'd set her afire like this, made her want him more than she'd ever wanted any man in her life.

"I think I'd better, honey," he soothed. "There is a lot unresolved between us and I want everything understood before I make you mine completely. I made that decision several days ago and I intend to stick to it. Otherwise I won't have any peace of mind left at all!"

"I...I don't understand," she breathed helplessly, feeling utterly bereft.

"I know you don't," he murmured gently. "That's why I'm calling a halt tonight. I've watched you all week, listened to your talk of starting a new life, seen you answer those employment letters while you lazed around my pool and kept an eagle eye on your relationship with Todd. You're driving me crazy, do you know that? It's like watching an intelligent, organized butterfly unfolding her wings and getting ready to fly off into the unknown with no thought of potential disaster."

She bit her lip, confused. Why was he talking

about the future? Wasn't he as consumed by the passion of the moment as she was?

"Don't you want me?"

"You're a woman, Lacey. You know the answer to that." The silvery eyes blazed for a moment and she thought she might have tipped the scales in her favor. Then she realized he had himself firmly back under control.

"We're in agreement on one thing at least, Lacey." He sighed. "Neither of us wants a one-night stand."

She stiffened at the words. Was that what tonight would have been? The cold words parted the mists of heightened desire and she began to return to earth. "What do you want, Holt?"

"It's a hell of a lot easier to tell you what I don't want!" he rasped. "And what I don't want is to begin a relationship with a woman who views me as the first in a chain of affairs which eventually is going to stretch all the way to Hawaii!"

His words came with measured cruelty, exerting a devastating effect. Lacey went white, staring at him as if he'd turned into a savage creature in front of her eyes.

"How dare you?" she flung at him, coming alive to struggle violently upright on the sofa. He watched enigmatically as she leaped to her feet, sliding the dress hastily over her head. Clothed once more she lifted her chin, glaring at him in the firelight. "You're making it sound as if I'm out to use you and every other man who takes my fancy!"

"Aren't you?" he murmured, lounging back against the cushions and eyeing her with a detached, vaguely critical expression that enraged her. "Are you going to stand there and claim that you intended to start anything more than a summer fling by going to bed with me tonight?"

Fury closed her hands into fists at her sides as she acknowledged to herself that she hadn't even thought that far ahead. When he held her, kissed her, all she had been able to think about were the shimmering waves of desire, the need to please and be pleased. The future hadn't entered her mind.

Driven to justify herself, she gritted her teeth. "What if that's true? Surely you're not going to claim you wanted anything more from me?"

He was on his feet with an explosion of movement that startled her, forcing her back a pace.

"What if I did?" he charged menacingly.

Confusion battled with anger. "If you did want something more? Holt, you can't mean you wanted anything else between us!"

"But that's exactly what I meant," he said with abrupt calm, the tension evaporating from his body as he faced her.

Lacey wondered if she'd heard him correctly. "But we hardly know each other, that is..." The protest died away at the look in his eyes.

"I learned long ago to recognize what I want in life, Lacey." Holt smiled strangely. "I want you, but I don't intend to be the first in a long line of short-lived, experimental relationships. An affair with me isn't going to be the casual, easily terminated business you say you intend to pursue."

"What *do* you want from me?" she tried to say coolly, her mind whirling.

"A commitment," he shot back feelingly, running a hand through his hair in a small gesture of exasperation. He stepped over to the fire, staring down into it moodily. "I don't want to wonder every time we argue if this will be the time you decide you can't be bothered to hang around and work out the problem. I don't want to watch you surveying the other men and wonder if you're thinking you'll find more excitement and romance with them. I don't want to watch you sitting around my pool all summer blithely answering job inquiries which could take you thousands of miles away at a moment's notice!"

She turned to stare at his hard profile etched in the firelight, feeling appalled. Put like that she sounded as if she were structuring a superficial, heartless life-style. He made her sound flighty, cruel and selfish. As cruel and selfish as his ex-fiancée had been? "You don't understand," she managed, feeing dazed by the turn of events.

"You keep saying that, but it's not true." The

words were soft but she heard the ghost of an indulgent smile in them which rekindled some of the annoyance he could elicit so easily in her. This was Holt in the pompous, superior attitude which reminded her so much of what she wanted to leave behind.

"It must be true," she countered gamely. "If you really understood what I'm trying to do with my life you wouldn't be implying such terrible things about me!"

"I'll take it as a positive sign that you do consider the implications terrible," he returned mildly.

"Now, you listen to me, Holt Randolph! You're the one who invited me out to dinner tonight. If you don't approve of my company, you shouldn't be keeping it!"

He swung around to face her, the light gleaming off his naked shoulders. Lacey swallowed a hint of uncertainty. He seemed very large and not a little intimidating in the confines of the cottage. "All I'm trying to say, Lacey," he ground out deliberately, "is that if we start an affair, it's not going to be the easy, uncomplicated arrangement you seem to think you want. If you get involved with me, you can count on being thoroughly entangled in my life. Think about it."

She glowered at him, momentarily speechless at his audacity.

"Don't look so shocked." He grinned suddenly,

stepping forward to frame her face between warm, rough palms. "I've been thinking about this all week and I believe it's going to work out. But you need a little time to readjust your thinking. You can still play the role of emerging butterfly, honey, but you'll have to redefine some of your goals...."

"Why, you pompous, egotistical, arrogant idiot! What in hell makes you think I'd bother to redefine *anything* for you!"

The grin turned wicked as he bent to brush her mouth lightly with his own. "Because you're going to find the new goals much more satisfying. What do you think we just proved there on the couch? You can't hide your response, sweetheart. You want me as much as I want you. But I intend to start this affair properly. I won't have you going into it thinking you can walk away when something more interesting comes along like a job in Hawaii or a man who fits your preconceived image of the perfect lover!"

"Good night, Holt!" Lacey's eyes flared almost green. "Thank you for a very *amusing* evening. I'm sure I shall remember it occasionally in Hawaii! Kindly remove yourself from my cottage!"

He went, somewhat to her surprise. She watched him stride calmly out the door and wondered at the new kind of restlessness he left in his wake.

The feeling was akin to what had driven her out

of Iowa but instead of the vague dissatisfaction, this time it had a definite focal point.

Who did he think he was to tell her she should change the whole direction of her life for the sake of an affair with the owner of Randolph inn? What made him think she wanted an affair with him in the first place?

She winced as her glance strayed to the telltale imprint of their bodies on the cushions of the sofa. Little fool that she was, she had given him the answer to *that* question with her response!

Anyone could get carried away once in a while, Lacey told herself bitterly. It didn't mean anything. Except that it had never happened quite that way before in her life, she was forced to tack on in a flash of honesty.

Damn it! Why did it have to be with Holt Randolph? Why couldn't it have been like that with Jeremy Todd or one of the other guests at the inn?

Her teeth snapping closed against the unanswerable question, Lacey stamped into the bedroom. A good night's sleep would undoubtedly help settle her mind.

But a good night's sleep quickly proved elusive. She was still awake an hour later, frowning darkly at the shadows on the ceiling and trying to think about the various job prospects she'd received so far when the tiny pebbles sounded playfully against her window.

It startled her. Lacey sat up, the frown turning to wary caution as she edged silently out of bed. Her ankle-length, dark green nightgown floated gracefully around her feet as she slipped along the wall and peered out the window from behind the curtain.

"Jeremy!"

With a laughing protest that was half relief, Lacey raised the window to find her friend standing outside, dressed in his jeans and a leather jacket.

"Hi!" He grinned.

"What are you doing here?"

"I came by to see if you wanted to go swimming." He indicated the towel draped around his neck.

"You've been drinking!" she accused.

"That's all there was to do tonight until you got back from your date with Randolph!"

"What about that blonde from Portland?" Lacey teased.

"I struck out. Turns out her husband is joining her here tomorrow. So give me an answer before we both freeze. Want to go for a swim? It will be like a bathtub in the pool room tonight!"

"There's a sign on the door that says no swimming after ten o'clock," she reminded him firmly. "It disturbs sleeping guests." It was almost two in the morning she realized, glancing at the clock beside her bed.

"No one will know. We'll be quiet about it.

Come on, Lacey. It'll be fun. We'll have the place to ourselves!''

She hesitated. Why was she waiting? It *would* be fun. And a swim might serve to relax her so she could get some sleep tonight. "I'll get my suit," she agreed in a rush, dropping the curtain. She thought she heard him mutter something like "spoilsport" just before she shut the window.

A short time later they crept into the silent, darkened pool area, feeling ridiculously adventuresome.

"Do you think we'll be shot at dawn if we're caught?" Lacey joked, stepping out of the jeans she'd thrown on over her swimsuit.

"Shoot a paying guest? Don't be ridiculous. Besides the rule about swimming after hours is mainly to keep rowdy drunks from drowning themselves or waking the other guests. We're not going to do either."

"You know, this may have been one of your brighter ideas, Jeremy," Lacey admitted as she floated peacefully on her back a few minutes later. He had been right. It did feel as if she were in a giant, indoor bathtub.

"Thanks, but it's mainly an excuse to do some research." He chuckled from a short distance away. "I'm going to put a scene like this in the next chapter of my book. With a few variations, naturally."

"What kind of variations?" Lacey closed her eyes and allowed herself to drift.

"Well," he began, swimming close behind her. "I'll be introducing a bit of sex into it...."

Lacey's eyes opened just as his mouth came playfully, hopefully down on hers.

She barely had time to ponder the difference between his kisses and the ones she had received earlier from Holt when the overhead lights snapped on, flooding the room with glaring brilliance.

"What the hell...?" Jeremy broke away from her as Lacey struggled to find her feet in the shallow water. They both turned to stare at the tall figure lounging in the doorway, arms folded across his chest.

"Oh, it's you, Randolph," Jeremy chuckled wryly. "You gave us a scare."

"Sorry to spoil the fun," Holt said evenly, his eyes burning over Lacey's figure. "But the rules apply to everyone, I'm afraid."

He was furious, Lacey realized. She could feel the waves of his anger lapping across the space which separated them, see the icy metal of the silvery eyes. He was furious with her. She knew as surely as if she could read his mind that he was barely restraining an urge to haul her bodily out of the water and wrap his fingers around her throat. She felt very naked and vulnerable standing there in the water.

Jeremy was shrugging philosophically. "Come

on, Lacey. It was fun while it lasted. But all good things come to an end.''

Wrenching her wide-eyed gaze away from Holt's pinning stare, Lacey turned to follow Jeremy out of the water. She reached for her towel as soon as she got to the top of the steps, the desire to cover herself paramount. She yanked off the bathing cap and let her hair swing loose.

''We'll go peacefully, Holt.'' Jeremy grinned good-naturedly, drying himself vigorously.

''*You'll* go peacefully,'' Holt replied, dislodging himself from the doorway and starting forward. ''I'll see Lacey back to her cottage.''

She glanced up anxiously. ''That won't be necessary. It's only a short distance and I...'' She broke off at the expression in his eyes.

He didn't bother to argue, waiting with ill-concealed impatience as they quickly gathered their clothes.

''It's going to be a cold dash back to the cottage.'' Jeremy sighed as he left them with an apologetic glance at Lacey. ''I'll see you tomorrow, Lacey.'' He loped quickly away as they exited the building.

''Holt, I can find my own way back, you don't need to escort me,'' she began quickly, edging toward the path without waiting for him.

He took her arm forcibly, causing her to clutch

at the towel. The cold night air bit at her bare legs and arms.

"I know you're not given to taking advice these days, Lacey," he snarled softly in the darkness as he hurried her briskly up the path. "But you'll ignore this piece of wisdom at your own peril. I'm giving you fair warning, don't say another word until we get to the cottage or I'll lose my temper completely. It's only hanging by a thread as it is!"

"Holt...!"

"I mean it, Lacey," he gritted.

She disregarded the advice in favor of stating her case and trying to gain some control over the situation. "Holt, listen to me! I'm sorry we broke your silly rule about swimming after hours, but there was certainly no harm done and I..."

"No harm done!" He slammed to a halt in the middle of the path, pulling her around to face him. In the moonlight his features took on the cast of an avenging demon. "No harm done! My God! What kind of woman are you? Only an hour ago you were lying in my arms, pleading with me to make love to you! The next thing I know you're seducing some other man in my swimming pool! I ought to break your neck!"

She flinched as his fingers sank into her naked shoulders. "Holt, please, you don't understand...." She was growing frightened. The anger in him was a seething fire ready to flare out of control and she didn't know how to placate him.

"You're always saying that!" He gave her a small, bruising shake. "And I'm beginning to think you might be right! I didn't understand earlier. I thought there was plenty of time left to reason with you but you've convinced me there isn't. We'll do things your way. You wanted an affair, Lacey Seldon; very well, you'll have an affair. With me. And it's going to begin tonight!"

Too late Lacey read the danger in him. Hastily she tried to step back out of reach but he moved too quickly, scooping her up into his arms and turning to stride toward the old Victorian-style summer home attached to the main lodge.

## Six

Regardless of the menace in Holt, Lacey's first reaction to being held tightly against his chest was one of relief. The warmth of his body warded off the chilling effects of the cold night breeze on her damp skin. Instinctively she wanted to nestle closer. But common sense shouted for attention and, out of habit, Lacey listened to it.

"Holt, you can't do this," she gasped, clutching her clothes to her as he carried her over the graveled walk and toward a short flight of steps.

"Not very long ago you were begging me to do it!"

"You're the one who called a halt back in my cottage," she flung at him. "You can't just change your mind like this...."

"Why not?" he asked with a mocking reasonableness as he climbed the steps to the glassed-in front porch. He set her down while he opened the door but he didn't let go of her arm.

"Because...because all the reasons you gave me an hour ago are still valid!" she squeaked as he hustled her inside.

Lacey barely noticed the old-fashioned white wicker furniture and the hanging greenery which filled the shadowy porch. Even had she chosen to study her surroundings there wasn't time to do so. She was firmly led across the sun porch and into the house.

"Listen to who's trying to argue rationally now!" Holt turned her into his arms as he closed the door behind them and switched on a light. "But it's too late for the rational, reasonable approach, Lacey; you've convinced me of that. You're determined to try the wild side of life. Why shouldn't I oblige? Why should I stand back and watch you try your experiments on Todd?"

"That's not what was happening!" she protested, collecting her anger as a defense. In the light of the hall lamp Holt looked hard and determined. The silvery-hazel eyes were almost metallic and the grim lines etching his mouth told his inner tension. Lacey trembled beneath his hands and it wasn't from the cold.

"Come on," he said abruptly as he felt the small

convulsion rack her body. "I don't want you catching a chill on the first night of our affair!"

One hand on the nape of her neck, he urged her through a living room that, under normal circumstances, would have fascinated her. Preoccupied as she was with the threat of the moment, however, she had only a fleeting impression of a gracious, masculine room which could have belonged to a nineteenth-century sea captain.

Beneath her feet an old and elegant oriental carpet covered a large section of the polished wooden floors. Out of the corner of her eye she spotted an antique seaman's chest with brass fittings. Fleetingly her mind catalogued a variety of exotic items: a beautifully worked silver bowl which had probably come from Mexico, a wall hanging with a Caribbean motif, a huge screen with an oriental design. All of them set amid dark, comfortable-looking wood and leather furniture.

"Holt, this has gone far enough," Lacey managed, as she found herself being dragged into a huge, surprisingly modern bathroom. "I know you're upset, although you have no reason to be, but I don't intend to allow you to take out your anger on me!"

He halted in the middle of the floor, snagging a striped towel from a nearby rack. "Here, wrap this around your hair," he ordered gruffly, handing it to her. "Give me those things," he added, taking the clothes she was still clutching protectively.

"What...what are you going to do?" she demanded a little weakly.

"Get you under a hot shower, naturally."

He reached behind the shower curtain and began adjusting knobs. "You're freezing and I have no desire to take an ice cube to bed tonight."

Lacey glared at him for an instant and then realized the shower would not only warm her up but would also give Holt a chance to cool off. She'd had plenty of opportunity to witness his restraint during the past week. Given a little breathing space, that trait would undoubtedly reassert itself.

Without further argument, she wrapped the towel around her hair and stepped into the shower, still wearing her swimsuit. The blast of hot water was wonderful.

If Holt was surprised at her sudden acquiescence, he didn't show it. Lacey had a brief glimpse of the silvery glitter in his eyes and then she firmly shut the shower curtain. She sensed his presence in the bathroom a moment longer and then she heard the door close behind him.

Now what? she asked herself grimly, turning beneath the hot water. How long would it take for him to calm down sufficiently to be reasonable? On the heels of that practical thought came another, very crazy realization. Did she really want him to be reasonable tonight?

Memories of the evening floated through her mind. The look in his eyes as he'd watched her at the dinner table, the warmth in him when he'd taken her in his arms, the promise in his lovemaking....

An unfulfilled promise, she reminded herself shakily. Unfulfilled because Holt had wanted a woman who would agree to his terms. He claimed he wanted nothing to do with a female embarking on a course of adventure.

She tried to tell herself that neither of them was suited to the other. Their feelings toward each other were too ambivalent, too at odds with what their rational thought process dictated. They were heading in opposite directions in life and any affair between the two of them would be fleeting at best.

But it wouldn't be a one-night stand, Lacey told herself resolutely. She would be here for the summer. Wasn't that long enough for the sort of relationship she'd planned for herself? That, of course, was assuming Holt was equally willing to go along with a summer affair. Earlier that evening he'd implied a relationship with a predetermined ending wasn't for him. He wanted a commitment. But neither of them wanted a one-night fling. Perhaps there was a middle ground....

The door to the bathroom opened.

"Planning on staying in there for the rest of the night?" Holt drawled.

Something in his voice brought Lacey back to reality in a hurry. He no longer sounded angry but neither did he sound as if he'd returned to the restrained, cautious mood she'd half expected. This new aspect ruffled her already heightened sense of awareness, caught at the threads of desire she'd tried to cool in the swimming pool. And, deep down, it sent prickles of a very primitive, very feminine alarm through her.

"I'll...I'll be out in a few minutes," she responded evasively, acutely awake to the new uneasiness he elicited in her. Fantasies of an exciting summer affair with this man suddenly dimmed only to be replaced by a strange caution.

"Don't rush," he murmured, sweeping back the curtain and raking her still-clothed body with a hungry, intent glance. "I'll join you."

"No!" Automatically Lacey put out a hand to stop him. His shirt was off and his hands were already going to the buckle of his belt. "I'll get out, Holt...."

It was too late. He was out of his garments and stepping into the shower before she could think of an argument to stop him. The uncompromising masculinity of him made her turn her head away from the lean, bronzed body. She moved backward a step, coming up against the white wall of the shower.

"What's the matter, Lacey?" he rasped softly, reaching out to pull her close as the water beat down on them. "Do you need a little help in getting your new life-style off the ground? Let me show you how it's done."

He tilted her chin and slowly, mesmerizingly lowered his head. Lacey's fingers curled into her palms and her eyes squeezed shut against the reality of what was happening. Her reservations and arguments both for and against an affair with Holt Randolph began to evaporate, leaving only a sense of the inevitable.

She stood very still as his lips brushed her closed eyes and then traced little patterns across her slickly wet skin to the edge of her cheek.

"It's not hard at all, Lacey," he gritted, sliding one hand down her slender back to the base of her spine. "The trick is to forget about tomorrow and the rest of your future. You live for the moment and learn to take what's offered. You'll get the hang of it. You're already convinced it's what you want, aren't you?"

"Holt, please..." Her voice was a shadowy, breathless sound. "I don't want a one-night stand. You know that...." She drew in her breath as he urged her lower body closer to his own. His hair-roughened thigh pressed against her with a kind of insistent, gentle aggression.

"It won't be a one-night affair. We have the summer, remember? As I recall, that should be all the sense of future you need to satisfy the remnants of your small-town conscience."

He was right, she tried to tell herself, but something in his voice mocked her. She felt his teeth nip gently at the lobe of her ear and then the warmth of the tip of his tongue as it found the shell-shaped interior. It was hotter than the water cascading over her body.

"You forced us both into a decision tonight, my reckless little Lacey. But that's the nature of the kind of life you want. Instant decisions and instant gratification. I told you earlier this evening that I know something about this sort of thing. Relax. I'll be happy to show you how it works...."

"But you don't approve of me!" she wailed as his fingers went to work on the fastening of the swimsuit. She pressed her face into his shoulder, her hands coming up to splay across his chest.

"I approve wholeheartedly about certain aspects of you." He chuckled deeply. "Don't worry about that!"

Her nails sank slightly into his skin as she felt the bathing suit stripped slowly, sensually down to her waist. The touch of his hands and the feel of his body were rapidly reviving all the restless need she had known earlier that evening. This was what she wanted, wasn't it? This undisguised passion and desire were the qualities she had been missing in her life. It was being offered to her at last. Only a fool would turn it down.

"Holt, do you love me a...a little?" She could have bitten her tongue as soon as the words left her mouth. That wasn't what she had meant to say at all! Where had the stupid, vulnerable words come from?

She felt him stiffen for a few seconds, felt his hands tighten at her waist and then he relaxed, nibbling sexily at the nape of her neck and the curve of her shoulder.

"Love you? That's the wrong question, Lacey," he told her relentlessly. "That's the sort of question you might ask a man back in Iowa. Not out here. The answer is, I want you."

And that should be enough, Lacey told herself resolutely. It was all that was necessary in an affair. Want and need. Passion and desire. Anything else was a sham, anyway. Hadn't she learned that by now? Men like Roger Wesley and the psych professor had talked of love and it had meant nothing. No, this was what she was looking for. Why did she hesitate?

She wound her arms around his neck with a soft sigh, piercingly aware of the feel of curling hair on his chest as it grazed her nipples. With a quick, gliding movement, the swimsuit was tugged down over her hips, falling to her feet. Holt groaned and molded her to him with fierce satisfaction.

Beneath the spray of the water, Lacey let all thought of the future slip away. This was what she wanted, what she had been longing for her entire life. She had come so far to find exactly these sensations, she reminded herself. Only a fool would get cold feet now.

She found the curving muscles of his back with probing, kneading fingers even as Holt began to shape her curves. She sensed his flaring arousal and took a deep pleasure in the knowledge that she could excite him as much as he excited her. It made her bolder, more adventuresome than she would ever have given herself credit for back in Iowa!

"I was an idiot to walk away from this earlier tonight," Holt muttered hoarsely, pinning her hips briefly against his and letting her know the fullness of his need. "If you're so bent on finding satisfaction with a man, why shouldn't it be with me?"

She wondered mistily if he was still trying to talk himself into taking her to bed and then dismissed the idea. He was as aroused and intent as she was. Neither of them wanted to call a halt now.

She felt his hands gliding up to cup her breasts and moaned softly, far back in her throat. Her head fell onto his shoulder in a small gesture of surrender and need. His lips caressed her throat as his thumbs gently worked circles around the erect nipples.

"Those men back in Iowa must have been cretins to let you slip away," he marveled. "How could any man resist the excitement in you?"

Lacey didn't know how to tell him that she had never felt this kind of excitement with any other man. So she contented herself with the thrill of holding him closer and finding the male nipples with her own lips.

She heard his indrawn breath, felt the surging desire in him, and knew it was echoed in herself. Her hands bit almost violently into the flesh of his lean waist and then they began to seek lower.

"My God, woman! You're enough to drive a man crazy!"

He released her breasts to find the gentle curve of her stomach and the roundness of her bottom. He arched her against him, forcing her head even farther back. Lacey experienced the delicious abandon and gave herself up to it. Time passed without meaning as they tasted and explored each other's bodies and then, with a suddenness that made her flick open her lashes, Holt reached out and shut off the water.

She met his now-burning gaze and it acted as another kind of caress on her already heated skin. Without a word he guided her out of the shower and into a thick bath sheet. Holt's eyes never left hers as he dried her with slow, passionate movements that left her knees feeling weak.

"Your turn," he whispered coaxingly, removing the towel and handing it to her.

Shakily she began to return the favor, rubbing the towel at first briskly and then more and more slowly. She knelt to dry his thighs and felt him unwrap the towel which had protected her hair. The auburn tresses fell around her shoulders and he wound his hands deeply into the tousled fire.

When she stood up slowly in front of him, he waited no longer. Lifting her high against his chest he carried her from the steamy bath out into the carpeted hall.

Lacey clung to him, one arm around his neck as Holt strode through an open door and into a darkened bedroom. A huge, four-poster bed dominated the shadowy scene, and Lacey was stood momentarily on her feet beside it while Holt tugged back the covers. Then he turned to look at her, not touching her.

"Come to my bed, my little adventuress. Let me give you what you're looking for. I want you so desperately tonight...."

"Yes," she whispered, lifting her arms to encircle his neck. "And I want you. Oh, Holt, I never dreamed I could want anyone so much...."

He slid her into bed and followed, pulling her

close to his straining body, shaping every inch of her with his hands.

Lacey felt as though she were melting into a molten figure of sensuality and need. His touch brought forth a level of desire she could not have guessed existed. And as she tasted it more and more deeply she knew beyond a doubt it was what she had been seeking.

"You're like hot quicksilver against my body," he breathed thickly, his fingers clenching erotically into the skin of her hip. Slowly he worked his way down her body while she twisted beneath him. When she felt his teeth on the vulnerable inside of her thigh she cried out softly.

Her response seemed to trigger an even greater one in him. He cupped her hips in both hands, raining scorching little kisses over the skin of her stomach and thighs until she thought she could bear no more.

When at last he moved higher, finding her breasts with his lips, Lacey gave into the urgency driving her. With a desperate little effort to which he acquiesced with a groan, she reversed their positions.

And then she was covering him with damp, lingering caresses, her hair strewn across his chest.

With delicate, passionate greed she enveloped Holt in a cocoon of soft femininity, pouring kisses across his shoulders, his chest, and his thighs. When she nibbled enticingly at his hip, her hands playing gently across him, she felt the ravaging need which shook him and caused his fingers to twist tightly into her hair.

"We must have been fated to meet like this," he ground out passionately.

"Yes," she agreed wonderingly, lost in the world of pure sensation. "Yes. This is what I wanted...."

"What you came to find? I'll make it perfect for you, just as you're making it perfect for me."

His words seemed a vow of desire and promise. He reached down and pulled her up beside him again, crushing her softly back into the bedclothes as if he could no longer wait to once again be the aggressor.

For long, passion-filled moments he continued to bring her senses to a pitch of awareness and need that amazed her. She was vaguely conscious of the brief moment when he moved away from her to assume the responsibility of taking precautions. She knew a surge of gratitude and even greater pleasure as she realized his care of her, and then she was once again drowning in his embrace.

"Holt, I don't think I can stand it any longer," she finally begged, clinging to him with all her might. "Please come to me. I must know where all this leads. I want you so badly...."

"I told you earlier what it does to me to have

you pleading like this," he said huskily. "We'll find out together where the ending lies...."

His leg moved heavily, insistently against her, parting her thighs and making a warm, heated nest for himself against her body. She cried out again as he moved on her, heard his answering groan and then they were both caught up in the deep, demanding rhythms of passion and desire.

Time stopped for Lacey as she moved into another plane of existence with the lover she had come so far to find. She knew beyond any shadow of a doubt that this was what had drawn her out of Iowa. How could she have resisted this feeling of being fully alive and totally involved with a man?

The surging, spiraling pattern carried them higher and higher, tossing them into the ultimate ending with a suddenness that brought a sob of wonder and exquisite satisfaction from Lacey. As if he had only been waiting for her to find the threshold, Holt gasped hoarsely, his face buried in the curve of her shoulder, his hands holding her to him with incredible strength.

Down, down they came on the other side of the magic doorway, clinging to each other as if to the only reality in their universe. Lacey's breath came in quick little gasps that slowly became fully relaxed and deeply satisfied.

She held Holt as all the masculine tension went

out of him. He covered her body with his hardness, giving himself up to her in the aftermath of desire.

For long moments they lay together in the damp, tangled warmth. Lacey's fingers trailed lightly, wonderingly, over Holt's sinewy back, delighting in the heaviness of him. She could think of nothing except the present.

At long last he stirred reluctantly, lifting his head to meet her love-softened eyes. In silence they regarded each other and then Holt said simply, meaningfully, "Was it what you were looking for?"

"Oh, Holt, you must know the answer to that," she breathed softly, raising her hand to toy with his ruffled, tawny hair. "I've never known anything like it. I only dreamed that someday I would find something approaching this...."

A gleam of pure male satisfaction lit the silvery gaze. "I've got news for you, the feeling was mutual. I spent several years searching the world for it, and all the time I was fated to find it here at home...."

"Lucky you." She grinned mischievously. "I spent years searching for it at home and finally had to come looking!"

"Point granted," he murmured gently, bending his head for an instant to drop a quick, light kiss on her nose. "But maybe that's because Iowa wasn't meant to be your home. Perhaps this island was to be the place where you would find home."

She tilted her head on the pillow, slanting him a teasing gaze. "What? You're no longer in a hurry to pack me off to Iowa?"

"I never was in a hurry to send you back there. I just wanted to make sure you stopped here!" He grinned wickedly.

"And so I have." She sighed luxuriously. "I have the rest of the summer to find..." She broke off as she felt him go suddenly, savagely tense. "What's wrong, Holt?"

"What do you mean, the rest of the summer?" he grated.

She blinked, uncertain of his sudden change of mood. A little chill coursed down her spine, replacing the sensual warmth she had known a moment before. "You said..." she began awkwardly as his eyes narrowed. "You said that neither of us wanted a one-night fling...."

"So? I also said I didn't want to be part of some experiment on your part, Lacey. I don't want a relationship with a preordained ending which suits your game plan."

A slow kind of anger began to build in her as she absorbed the implications of his words. "Are you saying you tricked me? That you...you seduced me tonight, hoping I would forget about my plans for the future?"

"What happened tonight was totally unplanned until I caught you in the pool with Todd. Your own behavior drove me to settle matters so quickly. But now that it's done, you're not going to have everything your own way!''

''Neither are you!'' she gritted, beginning to push at his shoulders in an attempt to free herself. ''How dare you think you can control me with sex! That's what this was all about, wasn't it? You couldn't talk me into seeing the light and doing things your way so you tried to seduce me into it!''

''Lacey, you're becoming irrational,'' he began impatiently, ignoring her struggles. ''Calm down and listen to me. Neither of us can walk away from the other now. Don't you understand? What we have is something special. We've both admitted that. Surely you can't believe yourself capable of enjoying yourself like this for the summer and then blithely leaving for Hawaii or Los Angeles!''

''Why not?'' she challenged, infuriated by the evidence of his scheming. ''What makes you think you can change my whole life simply by taking me to bed? I told you I was only looking for a summer affair....'' The reckless words poured out of her, driven by anger and dismay at the trap she saw closing around her. She would not allow herself to be seduced into giving up all her carefully worked out plans. She knew what she wanted from life, didn't she?

''Lacey,'' he soothed, stroking her hair back from her face, his mouth grim. ''Hush, Lacey. Listen to me. I know things didn't go as either of us had planned tonight, but that doesn't mean…''

"Don't think you can sweet-talk me into doing things your way, Holt Randolph! Everyone I've ever known has assumed he or she could talk me into doing things their way. Well, I changed that. I make my own decisions now. I will not let someone else decide what's proper for me. Nor will I let you coerce me into doing what you want!''

"You're willing to do all the taking but none of the giving, is that it?'' he bit out a little savagely, propping himself up on his elbows and glaring down at her. "You're willing to sample some of the passion you've been searching for but you're not willing to pay for it with any kind of honest commitment…!''

"That's not true!'' she rasped, shocked at the escalating tension between them. This wasn't the way it should be, not after what they had just shared! Why was he ruining everything?

"It is true. You're still intent on dashing off the moment something more amusing or interesting takes your attention, aren't you? I told you, Lacey, you can't have everything your own way. That's not how matters are going to be between us. If you're not willing to give yourself up to an honest relationship without an arbitrary ending established by you, then I'm not willing to let myself be used in an experiment!''

"What are you saying?" she gasped furiously as he rolled off her body to sit up on the edge of the bed.

He turned his head to rake her sprawled form. "It's simple, really. I'd rather be used for one night than for a whole summer. The lesser of two evils, I guess you could say."

"You said...you said you didn't want something that only lasted a night!" she yelped protestingly, raising herself up to a sitting position and pulling the sheet to her throat. She stared at him, wide-eyed and suddenly, horribly apprehensive.

"I said I didn't want it, not that I couldn't handle it," he growled pointedly.

"I suppose that means you've had a lot of them, is that it?" She was blazing with anger. "You can *cope* with the situation because you've experienced it before!"

He shrugged with massive casualness, which only inflamed her further. "I can cope with it better than I can cope with the trauma of an affair which is doomed to end in a couple of months. You're not going to use me like that, Lacey."

"You don't understand...!"

"If you say that one more time tonight I'm going to turn a little savage!"

"Don't threaten me!"

"Like they say, it's not a threat, it's a promise. Get dressed, Lacey, I'm taking you back to the cottage." He surged to his feet, moving toward his closet with a determined stride. He paused en route to pick up her jeans and shirt from a nearby chair and hurl them at her in a soft wad.

She stared down at them blankly as they crumpled on the bed beside her and then lifted her head again as he spoke from the vicinity of the closet. "It's going to be interesting watching you learn how to deal with this kind of thing," he said with cold amusement as he tugged on a shirt. "Think of it as good experience. I'm sure there will be plenty of instances in the future when you'll find it useful. You have to expect a certain percentage of your affairs to wind up like this. That's part and parcel of your new life-style, honey. Comes with the territory."

# *Seven*

It was a restless, frustrating sense of anger which forced Lacey out of bed far earlier the next morning than she would normally have arisen after such a late night. But it was hopeless trying to sleep in when one's brain was literally seething, she decided wretchedly, throwing back the covers and heading for the bathroom.

How could she have been such a fool? How could she have let Holt take her to bed? Where had that stupid midwestern common sense been the one time in her life she could have used it?

It was no use trying to tell herself Holt had forced himself on her. He had been infuriated at finding her with Jeremy in the pool, but in spite of his threats, he would never have forced her into bed. Lacey knew that. She grimaced wryly in the mirror at the memory of her own desire.

No, she couldn't blame Holt for what had happened, though it would have given her a certain amount of pleasure to do so. She couldn't even blame him for wanting the affair conducted on his terms. All men wanted to be the ones who chose the ending point of a relationship.

Face it, she thought bitterly as she pulled on jeans and a loosely woven, bulky top, her anger was based on something far more potentially dangerous that Holt had done to her. Even now in the full light of morning she didn't want to think about it.

In the tiny kitchen she morosely went about the business of making coffee and forced herself to examine the real issue carefully. The unnerving, frightening thing that had happened last night had led to the compelling sense of commitment with which she had awakened this morning.

It was ridiculous, insane, some strange figment of her imagination, she decided as she sat at the little table by the window and stared into the coffee in her mug.

But even during her marriage she hadn't experienced such a sensation of being fundamentally bound to a man. With Roger her loyalty had been largely based on a sense of duty and, in the beginning, genuine affection. The affection had died rather quickly when she began to realize exactly what role she played in her husband's life. The sense of duty had remained until the divorce was final. It had been relatively easy to behave properly under the circumstances because there simply hadn't been much in the way of temptation back in Iowa!

But this intense, inexplicable feeling of being chained had nothing to do with duty or conscience. None of those factors was at work in her precarious relationship with Holt Randolph. Yet after one night in his bed she woke up with a sense of belonging.

It probably had something to do with the strength of the passion she had experienced, she told herself, leaping to her feet in annoyance to carry the mug over to the sink. But that didn't really explain things, either. Passion might conceivably make you crave a man but it wouldn't make you feel bound to him. Not the way she felt bound this morning.

Lacey paused in front of the sink, staring out the window without quite seeing the sweep of Puget Sound and the other islands in the distance. For a long moment the whole dazzling future she'd planned for herself danced in front of her eyes. How could she even think of pushing that future off into the distance and replacing it with a relationship with a man who had turned his back on everything she was seeking?

Lacey gritted her teeth. The fact that she could even ask the question was frightening in the extreme. She hadn't come all this way only to tie herself down to one man. A man who didn't even show any interest in living the sort of life-style she wanted. For heaven's sake, she thought grimly, living on this island for any extended period of time would have all the elements of small-town life in Iowa! She would be trapped again.

No, this island was merely a stopover on the way to her new life. Holt's lovemaking last night couldn't be allowed to change that. She had come too far, planned too long to give up her dreams because of one night in a man's arms.

Holt was right, Lacey thought determinedly. A woman had to expect a certain percentage of her affairs to wind up as one-night stands! It was her own fault. She should have made certain she and Holt were in agreement on the nature of their affair before she had allowed it to proceed.

Now what? She glanced out the window again, knowing she wasn't going to follow her usual early morning practice of meditation. Her mind was far too keyed up and besides, there was always the awkward possibility Holt might decide to indulge in his early morning habit of running. The thought of meeting him today was enough to make her shiver. What did you say to a man after a night like the one that had just passed?

She bit her lip reflectively, facing up to the situation fully. Could she even continue to stay on this island?

As soon as the thought occurred to her, Lacey realized she'd been pushing it to the back of her mind. But there it was: Wouldn't it be easier on herself to simply pack up and leave? How could she face the rest of the summer here? Every time she saw Holt she would think of last night.

A gleaming white Washington State Ferry came into view out on the Sound and Lacey suddenly decided what she was going to do that day. She needed to get away and think. What better escape than taking a small cruise?

The ferry schedule was tacked to a bulletin board in the lobby of the inn. Lacey hurried down the path toward the main building, trusting to luck she wouldn't run into Holt, and was relieved to find only George behind the desk. She smiled at the assistant.

"Good morning, George. I just came to check the ferry schedule. Is the mail in yet?"

"Just arrived, Lacey." He smiled cheerfully, bending down to retrieve a stack of white business envelopes and hand them to her. "Going for a little tour?" he added politely as she studied the schedule with a small frown.

"Yes, I feel like getting away today," she replied, forcing a smile as she reached out a hand to accept the stack of mail. ''I see there's one due in about thirty minutes. If I rush I might make it down to the docks.''

He nodded genially. ''Enjoy yourself!''

Lacey's mouth quirked wryly at the thought and then she was out the door, hurrying back toward the cottage and her car.

She made the ferry docks with a few minutes to spare. The small line of cars was soon boarded, and Lacey left her Fiat down on the car deck while she made her way up to the passenger rooms. She would have plenty of time to get another cup of coffee and plan the next leg of her trip before the ferry docked on the mainland. With a little timing, she could ride ferries all over the San Juans today!

She stood in line at the concession stand, obtained her coffee, and then headed out on deck. It was cool this morning and the breeze whipped her auburn hair lightly around her face. The hot coffee tasted good and the fresh air was invigorating. She had made the right decision. Leaning against the rail, she gazed reflectively at the multitude of green islands which dotted the inland sea.

Deliberately she tried to let her mind go blank, the way she did during meditations in the mornings. She needed to think logically and calmly about the situation in which she found herself. Lacey was trying to find a point of beginning for the intensely private discussion when all her carefully arranged sense of calm was shattered by a familiar, gravelly voice. Holt!

"Running away, Lacey?" he drawled behind her. "You surprise me. I thought midwesterners were famous for their stubborn determination."

She whirled, the coffee in her hand slopping precariously near the rim of the cup. "You followed me!" she accused.

He shrugged, not bothering to respond to the obvious and moved up beside her on the rail. He, too, was holding a cup of coffee and his tawny hair was attractively wind-ruffled. He was dressed in a pair of jeans and had thrown a light jacket over a long-sleeved shirt.

"Why?" she demanded starkly, unhappily aware of the little jerk of excitement she was experiencing at the mere sight of him. It was as if his very presence was enough to produce a small tug on the velvet bonds with which she felt bound. She might fight that sensation!

"To see if you really were running away," he replied easily, slanting her a very straight glance as he rested his arms on the railing. "George told me you were asking about ferry schedules, and when I saw your car leave I decided I'd tag along and point out a few facts of life."

"You already did that. Last night." She turned her head, refusing to meet his eyes.

"So that's the plan, hmmm? You're going to assume the role of the injured party?'' he taunted in a rough growl.

''Don't tell me you wanted that part!''

''Ah, but I did. I felt quite used, you know.''

Her eyes narrowed suspiciously. ''If you did, you have only yourself to blame.''

''Are you really going to have the audacity to stand there and tell me that what happened last night was entirely my fault?'' he murmured beside her.

Lacey swallowed, her hands tightening on the rail. ''You're the one who practically dragged me out of that pool and forced me to take that shower....''

''But I didn't drag you into bed, did I? You came quite willingly. Can't you at least be honest about that much, Lacey?''

She sucked in her breath and lifted her chin. ''Yes,'' she agreed steadily. ''I can be honest about that part. It was, in the final analysis, simply a matter of both of us succumbing to the moment. Which, translated, means we both made a mistake.''

''And now you're running away,'' he concluded in a flat tone.

''No.'' She shook her head. ''I only wanted time to think. I decided to spend some time hopping islands on the ferries.''

There was a pause beside her. ''While you go over your options?''

"Something like that."

"And running away is one of your options?" he persisted, making Lacey grit her teeth in frustration.

"Will you stop implying I'm some sort of coward! Doesn't it occur to you that my leaving might be the most sensible move under the circumstances? The easiest thing for both of us?"

"It wouldn't be." He sighed and took a sip of coffee.

"Why not?" she challenged, feeling pressured.

"Leaving isn't going to change what we have. You'll still be thinking about last night six months from now, just as I will."

She swung around to stare at him, aghast. "That's crazy!"

His mouth quirked a little crookedly. "I only wish it were. Take it from someone who's already gone the route you're trying to find. Last night was special. Very special. That's why I followed you this morning. I had to make sure you knew that."

"You said you could cope with it," she reminded him tersely, not wanting to admit the truth of what he said.

"I can if I have to, but I'd just as soon not. I want you, Lacey," he said heavily.

"You practically threw me out last night." She bit the words out scathingly, hiding her hurt beneath a wall of anger.

"I was madder than hell last night. You were so

damned obstinate! Still clinging to your dreams of a new life filled with adventure. Even after what we'd just shared. How do you think I felt afterward when you made it clear you saw me as just the start of your adventures?''

She flinched. ''How do you think I felt when you acted as if, having seduced me, everything was settled the way you wanted it? How do you think I felt having you dictating my future just like everyone else in my life has tried to dictate it? You want me to do things your way, have the affair your way. It's your ego which can't stand the thought of me calling a halt to the affair in September, isn't it? You want the power to do that. That's why you want an indefinite commitment from me!''

He stared at her, his expression hard and remote. ''Do you really believe that?''

She closed her eyes briefly against the force of his pride and willpower. ''I don't know,'' she said finally, her voice sounding forlorn, even to her own ears. ''I just don't know.''

His face softened and he lifted his hand to flick gentle fingers along the line of her cheek. ''Poor Lacey,'' he murmured, sounding half amused, half frustrated. ''Things aren't going quite the way you planned, are they? You've barely started pulling together the threads of a new life for yourself and already you're running into snags.''

He bent his head and kissed her warmly, lingeringly. She didn't try to evade the caress. When he raised his head again he was smiling ruefully. "Can't you trust me when I tell you that there's nothing waiting out there in your new life that will compare with what we've got between us?"

"But I won't know that for certain until I've found out for myself, will I?" she breathed, studying his face.

"Do you think I can wait for you? It wouldn't work, Lacey. I'd have nightmares wondering who you were with, worrying about how many risks you were taking. Give us a chance, honey. Make a commitment to what we have and if it doesn't work out you'll still be free to go your own way...."

"At some vague point in the future?"

He said nothing, waiting. She could feel him trying to compel her with every fiber of his will.

"Are you sure a full-fledged affair is what you want, Holt?" Lacey went on with an effort. "That island of yours if fairly small. Wouldn't you worry about what your neighbors and the guests would say? It would be like trying to conduct an affair back in my hometown!"

"Are you telling me you want marriage?" he said with deceptive casualness.

She stepped backward abruptly, appalled. "No! Of course not! Marriage is the last thing I want!"

"So you've implied on a number of occasions. Okay, I accept that. I can tolerate the talk on the island but I won't tolerate being used. You want me as much as I want you, Lacey. All I'm asking for is a compromise. Give me your word that you'll give our relationship a fair chance. Promise me you won't spend every waking minute planning a future that doesn't include me and I'll..." He broke off suddenly.

"You'll what, Holt? What do you have to offer in exchange for my postponing the future?" she hissed.

"A present that's better than the future will ever be," he said simply.

"I'll only have your word for that."

He shook his head firmly. "No. There will come a time when you'll know for certain that what you've found is what you were really looking for all along."

She eyed him with sudden intuition. "Is that how it was for you?"

He smiled. "Want to hear about it?"

"You're trying to dangle a lure in front of me. You know I want to hear the rest of your story!"

"Well, since we seem to be committed to a ferry ride..."

"Several of them!" she interposed briskly. "I'm not going back to the cottage until I've had a chance to think about what I'm going to do."

"Since we seem to be committed to *several* ferry rides," he amended meekly, "why don't you come inside out of this wind and I'll give you the second half of my life story?''

Lacey struggled mentally for a long moment, telling herself she needed to come to her own conclusions and not let herself be influenced. But it seemed ridiculous to deliberately avoid him on the small ferry. And she did want to hear the story of how he'd wound up on his island running the family inn when he'd had a life that had offered so much more.

They sat across from each other on padded seats near the massive ferry windows and Lacey listened politely for a few moments while Holt gave her the names of some of the islands floating past. But when his comments threatened to turn into a tour-guide monologue, she interrupted coolly.

"You promised, Holt," she murmured.

"So I did," he admitted reluctantly, settling back against the seat cushion. "Let's see, where did I leave off...?"

"You were happily enjoying the exciting life, traveling from place to place and supervising the start-up of new hotels," she prompted dryly.

"Oh, yes. Living the good life..." he mocked.

"Wasn't it?" she pressed laconically. "Or are you going to sit there and give me a lecture on the evils of the fast life?"

"It had its moments."

"I'll bet!"

"I wish you wouldn't look so enthusiastic," he said with a groan. "People like us go into that sort of existence because we're searching for something. But the answers are no more likely to be out there than they are anywhere else. The kind of life is not a goal in itself, Lacey, can't you understand that? It's a place to go hunting when you've exhausted other possibilities, but if you've already got what you need back home, it's a waste of time...."

"What I need isn't back home!" she declared tightly.

"I'm not saying it is. I fully agree that you've given Iowa its chance!" He chuckled ruefully.

"But not your island?" she concluded promptly.

"Or me."

"I gave you a chance last night," she retorted flippantly. "And you kicked me out when you decided I didn't measure up."

"Lacey!" He leaned forward with unexpected swiftness, grasping her small-boned wrist and freezing her with the glitter in his eyes. "Don't say that, dammit! You were the one using me last night and don't you forget it! My God! At one point you even wanted me to admit I loved you! That would have made me a very nice notch on your bedpost, wouldn't it?"

"I never meant it like that!" She gasped, alarmed at his intensity. "I don't even know what made me say it. Old...old habits die hard, I suppose...."

"Old habits like expecting the man to say he loves you before he takes you to bed?" he mocked gently. "Don't worry, you'll get over that eccentricity in a hurry if you follow the path you're so determined on pursuing."

"We're straying from the subject," she ground out furiously.

"So we are." He sat back, the ice in his eyes melting slowly. "I think I was in Acapulco when I got word my grandfather was dying," he said crisply. "I came back to say good-bye. I loved him, even if we hadn't been able to agree on my career."

He paused and Lacey's natural sympathy softened her anger as she watched the memories flit through his eyes.

"He died soon after I arrived in Seattle, and as I stood at the funeral I could practically feel all my relatives assuming that now I was home to stay." Holt shook his head wryly. "No one said anything, they just *expected* me to do the right thing."

"Which was to take over the inn?"

"Correct. Grandfather had very neatly tightened the knot by willing the whole business to me. I either had to run it or sell it. I went over to the island to take a look at the place and see if I could estimate how much it might bring."

"You intended to sell?"

He nodded. "As far as I was concerned, as soon as I'd settled the fate of the inn, I was going back to Acapulco. When I arrived on the island I was shocked at the condition of the place. I hadn't seen it for several years and granddad had let it run down terribly. I couldn't believe it. I kept walking around the gardens and through the buildings remembering how it had been in its heyday. Then I started thinking about all the changes and improvements I had once envisioned making on the place."

"So you got hooked and decided to stay?" Lacey asked curiously.

"Not exactly. I decided to fix the place up so that I could get a good price for it. I'd learned a lot about modern innkeeping while working for the hotel chain. I also had a lot of my own ideas. I told myself I could double the asking price of the inn if I put in a few improvements. Well, one thing led to another and finally one day it dawned on me I never intended to sell. I took a good look at what I was doing and realized I'd gone far beyond what would have been necessary for resale purposes. I also realized I wasn't missing my old life one bit."

"So you accepted the chains the family had put on you, after all," Lacey murmured.

"Nothing that dramatic," he retorted with a cool glance. "I'd found what I wanted to do in life. I would have been a fool to go back to my old life in search of the satisfaction I had found at home."

"What, exactly, is the moral of this little story?" Lacey demanded, frowning.

"I got lucky, Lacey. Circumstances brought me back for another look at what I'd turned down a few years earlier. And the second time around I had the sense to recognize I'd found what I wanted. But life doesn't always provide neat second opportunities like that. If you walk out on what we've got without even giving it an honest chance, you won't get a second one!"

"You've already told me you won't wait until I sow my wild oats," she retorted. "I feel duly warned." But it was becoming increasingly difficult to maintain the flippant defiance and Holt must have seen it because his response was a knowing smile.

"I'm offering you a chance to sow them with me. I just don't want to be tossed aside when you're ready for a new adventure."

Lacey's hostility collapsed beneath the weight of her conscience. "Holt, I never meant to hurt you or mislead you. I've tried to be very straightforward since the beginning," she murmured urgently, her eyes full of a gentle remorse.

"But you weren't honest and straightforward last night, honey," he interrupted meaningfully. "You told me one thing physically and quite another verbally."

"That's not true!"

"It is true," he argued. "Why do you think I got so angry I made the mistake of taking you back to the cottage instead of keeping you in my bed? You gave yourself to me as if I were the only man on earth who mattered at all to you. And then, when it was over, you still talked of leaving at the end of the summer. I told you I was going to let you find out what it was like to participate in a one-night stand because it was the only way I had of retaliating for what you were doing to me...."

"You were very cruel!"

"So were you. But I'm prepared to accept the responsibility for handling things all wrong last night. It was too soon and I knew it. My only excuse is that after finding you in the pool with Jeremy my instincts were racing ahead of my common sense." He sighed. "And then, when you insisted on arguing with me instead of bowing before my masculine ire, I lost my head and decided to show you what you were missing by wasting your time on Todd!" The wry humor was heavily overlaid with self-disgust.

"Is this an apology?" she managed with a small attempt to lighten the atmosphere between them.

"I suppose so. I only know I shouldn't have pushed you into that sort of a situation last night. You're an intelligent, strong-willed woman and you need to come to the right conclusions on your own."

"Thank you!" she snapped a little huffily.

"I'm not being condescending," he protested quickly.

"Aren't you?"

"No. Well, perhaps, a little. But only because…"

"You know what's best for me?" she concluded sweetly.

"Damn right," he retorted without batting an eye. "And one of these days you're going to realize it! Now, which island are we heading for next?"

She blinked at the change of topic. "I don't know. I…uh…was going to check the map near the main lounge…." Her words trailed off in confusion. "You're really planning on coming with me?"

"I have to find some way of apologizing for kicking you out of bed last night, don't I?" he countered smoothly.

She felt the red stain her cheeks. "I'd rather we didn't discuss that any further."

"Your wish is my command. Come on, I'll point out the most interesting islands." He got to his feet and pulled her up beside him, striding briskly toward the main lounge. "I walked on board so we'll use your car."

Holt was determined to restore the balance between them, Lacey acknowledged as the day wore on. He was every inch the cheerful, attentive escort as they hopped on and off ferries until late in the afternoon. He took her to the myriad little arts-and-crafts boutiques sprinkled about the island villages, entertained her over a delicious lunch of steamed crab and told her bits and pieces of the history of Puget Sound.

Slowly the wariness in her dissolved and she gave herself up to the pleasant day, feeling regret when it came to an end. Holt, who had automatically taken the wheel of the Fiat, drove the little car off the homeward-bound ferry and finally parked it sedately in front of her cottage.

"Well," he demanded lightly, his eyes serious as he turned in the seat to confront her. "Am I forgiven? Can we at least declare a functional truce?"

"You want things to go back to the way they were before last night?" Lacey asked quietly, searching his expression with sudden caution.

He hesitated. "I don't think that's possible, do you? I'm asking for a truce during which we can get to know each other better."

"During which you can convince me that your way is right and mine is wrong?"

"See? I told you that you were basically intelligent!"

She grinned in spite of herself. "I'm not going to run away if that's what you're afraid of. I've got too much crucial correspondence established with this address!"

"Thanks," he muttered disgustedly. "You mean you're staying because you don't want to risk having all your potential employers lose track of you at this juncture!"

Lacey's grin broadened cheerfully. "A touch of that midwestern practicality, I guess!"

But she knew that wasn't the truth. She was staying on the island because she couldn't bring herself to walk away from Holt Randolph just yet. Somehow the day she had spent with him had only tightened the velvet chains he had shackled her with last night.

She didn't know what to expect as she dressed for another evening with the crowd at the lodge. She only knew she couldn't stay away. Holt would call her a coward if she did. She would call herself a coward!

But while she didn't quite know what to expect, she was totally unprepared for the shock which awaited her as she slipped familiarly into the cheerful crowd sharing brandy and gossip.

The raven-haired beauty clinging so elegantly to Holt's arm could be none other than his ex-fiancée.

# Eight

"**S**he's a knockout, isn't she?" Jeremy Todd noted with a grin as he spotted Lacey standing at the edge of the group and moved to her side. He slanted an assessing, approving glance at the tall, sophisticated woman near the center of the room. "The name's Joanna Davis, according to Edith and Sam. The famous fiancée."

"*Ex*-fiancée, I believe you said," Lacey murmured, sipping at the glass of brandy Jeremy handed to her while she studied the other woman. Joanna Davis was, indeed, a knockout by most standards. Her black hair gleamed in an elegant chignon and her vivid blue eyes were sensuously veiled by sultry, sooty lashes. Her features were delicate and had the faintly aristocratic cast which lent a woman instant sophistication. Joanna had obviously capitalized on that natural gift. She was wearing a slender black sheath which added sheer drama to her looks. Something very brilliant gleamed at her throat and wrist. Mentally Lacey pegged her age at around thirty-two.

"A tad overdressed for this crowd, don't you think?" she couldn't resist remarking and immediately winced at the catty words.

Jeremy lifted one eyebrow in mocking comprehension. "So that's the way it is, hmmm? I'm not surprised," he added cheerfully.

"What are you talking about?"

"Relax. It's no secret you and Randolph disappeared together for most of the day. And I happen to know for a fact that you weren't hustled directly back to your cottage last night. I watched to see if your lights came on shortly after mine and they didn't."

"Are all writers so nosy?" she demanded, annoyed.

He quirked his mouth wryly. "It's okay, you know. You don't have to tell me we weren't exactly on the brink of a flaming affair!"

She stared at his unconcerned expression and burst out laughing. "Thanks a lot! You don't have to act that casual about matters! Have you no respect for my feminine ego? You could at least pretend to be mildly heartbroken!''

He chuckled. ''Sorry, but I learned to recognize a 'good friends' situation long ago. The only thing that puzzles me is I don't quite see you and Holt as a couple. What are you going to do when the Hawaiian job comes through?''

''Holt and I have had a couple of dates and that's the extent of matters,'' Lacey said firmly, lying through her teeth.

''You may be right, now that Joanna is back on the scene,'' Jeremy observed reflectively.

In spite of her determination not to do so, Lacey found herself flicking another glance toward the poised, aloofly smiling woman on Holt's arm. At that moment, Holt glanced up and saw her. She had an instant's impression of a glacial cold in his silvery hazel eyes and then it was gone and his eyes found hers. For a taut second they held each other's glances across the room and then Holt turned back to the woman at his side.

Lacey realized he was disentangling himself from Joanna Davis's embrace and felt a tingle of panic. He was obviously intent on heading toward her and Lacey wasn't quite sure how to handle the situation. She was saved from having to worry about an immediate response when one of the night clerks came through the door behind her and surveyed the crowd with an air of importance.

"Oh, there you are, Miss Seldon," the young man said hastily. "Telephone call for you. I thought you'd be in here so I didn't transfer it to your cottage. Want to take it in the lobby?"

"Thanks." She hurried into the quiet lobby with a sense of relief, even though the only place the phone call could be from at this time of night was Iowa.

"Hello?" She waited expectantly to hear her mother's voice and it was with a shock that she realized it was Roger Wesley on the other end of the line.

"Hello, Lacey," he murmured in what she assumed was his best bedside manner. "It's good to hear your voice again...."

"Oh, it's you, Roger. What in the world do you want?" she grumbled unenthusiastically.

There was a distinct silence as Roger assimilated her unencouraging response. She could practically see him choosing his words carefully. "Your parents gave me your number...."

"I can't imagine why."

"Now, darling," he soothed. "I know I hurt you two years ago but we were young...."

"Roger, please don't get maudlin. Say what you have to say and get off the phone. I'm busy."

"Darling, I understand that you're merely trying to protect your emotions with such defenses...."

"Roger, you don't happen to know a professor

in the psych department at the university, do you? Named Harold? Has a couple of kids?''

"What the devil are you talking about?'' Roger asked, displaying a tinge of irritation.

"Never mind. What do you want?''

"Darling, you know your family is worried about you,'' he began, the bedside manner now reflecting firmness and a doctor's sureness. Like everyone else back home, Roger Wesley always felt he knew what was best for Lacey.

"And they've asked you to talk me into going home?'' she interpreted astutely.

"They thought I could talk some sense into you, yes. Now calm down and listen to me, Lacey....''

"I assure you, I'm not particularly excited.''

"Your mother told you I'm getting a divorce?'' Roger went on, clearly searching for the human understanding he'd always been able to expect from Lacey.

"Yes,'' she admitted, turning to glance over her shoulder as the door behind her opened. Holt stood there.

"I want to talk to you about this decision, Lacey. It involves you. I've been thinking a lot about you lately and I...''

"Roger, I've got better things to do at the moment. Good night...''

"Lacey!''

"Roger, unless you want to get a bill from me

itemizing all those medical-school fees I paid, you'd better forget about pestering me!" Without waiting for a reply, she slammed down the receiver.

"This seems to be our night for hearing voices from the past," Holt drawled from the doorway.

"You appear to have a bit more than a disembodied voice calling to you from out of your past," she murmured sweetly.

"Oh, she has a body, all right," he agreed imperturbably. "I'd almost forgotten how much of one!"

Lacey gritted her teeth, alarmed at the unexpected anger which was welling up out of nowhere. "She clearly dressed tonight to bring back fond memories."

The enigmatic silvery gaze swept Lacey's white painter's shirt from its neckline to its full widecuffed sleeves. The drawstring neckline was open, revealing the line of her throat and shoulders but not the small swell of her breasts. She wore it with a gauzy, full skirt, and next to the slinky black outfit Joanna Davis had on, she felt as if she'd just stepped off the plane from Iowa.

"You're not jealous by any chance?" Holt asked interestedly.

"No," Lacey retorted icily. "I'm afraid that phone call put me in a bad mood. I..."

She was saved from whatever inane remark she

might make next as the door behind Holt opened again to reveal Joanna Davis.

"There you are, darling. I was wondering where you'd disappeared. The dancing has started in the lounge and it's been so long since we've danced together." The beautifully-made-up blue eyes flared with sultry memories, and Lacey found her nails digging into her palms. What was the matter with her? Why should this creature from Holt's past bother her?

"Of course, Joanna," Holt murmured, glancing down at the possessive fingers on the sleeve of his tan jacket. "I'll be right with you."

He turned as if he were about to say something more to Lacey and then Jeremy was cheerfully barging through the door.

"Come on, Lacey. Let's dance!" He started forward, ignoring the other two and grasped her wrist. "Randolph's booked a new band for tonight!"

Lacey smiled serenely at the other woman as she was hauled past but Joanna had the last word.

"There now, Holt. You won't have to worry about your little guest being properly entertained tonight. He looks just her type."

Jeremy let the door swing shut behind him, mopping his brow theatrically. "Wow! She's a knockout in more ways than one. Pure poison, if you ask me! I saw her following Randolph, who was going after you, and I decided to join the procession. Gallant, huh?''

"Very," Lacey said with a rueful smile.

"She certainly seems to be back here for one purpose and one purpose only," Jeremy went on, leading Lacey toward the darkened lounge.

"She's out to snag Holt again?" Lacey hazarded with a sigh.

"Edith and Sam are sure of it. And, frankly, he doesn't seem to be running too fast in the opposite direction."

Lacey thought about that remark several times during the evening. She danced frequently with Jeremy and with a few of the other guests, and every time she found herself on the dance floor it seemed Holt was there with his ex-fiancée. They made a handsome couple, she thought sadly. Couldn't Holt see the woman was a born user of men?

It was nearly eleven o'clock when Lacey glanced up in time to see Holt and Joanna approaching the table she shared with Jeremy.

"Here comes trouble," Jeremy said in a tone of deepest resignation. "What do you want to bet I'm about to have the privilege of dancing with sweet Joanna? Doesn't look too pleased at the prospect, does she?"

He had guessed accurately, as it turned out. Holt murmured some words about giving Joanna a break and letting her dance with Jeremy and the next thing Lacey knew she herself was in Holt's arms on the dance floor.

"What did Roger have to say?" he began without preamble, his hold on her surprisingly firm. It was a firmness that didn't reflect desire, only a restrained disapproval.

"He's been appointed to try and talk some sense into me," Lacey retorted lightly, wondering at Holt's mood. What was the matter with him? Was he jealous? It was he who had been entertaining an ex-fiancée all evening, not her!

"Will he succeed?" he asked crisply.

"I don't know. Will Miss David succeed in talking sense into you?"

He stiffened. "What, exactly, do you know about her?"

"Word travels fast in a small community," Lacey said with grim cheerfulness. "I know the two of you were once engaged, that Joanna has since been married and divorced and that speculation is running wild over the possible reasons for her presence here at the resort."

"I guess that about sums it up," he admitted dryly.

"Not quite," she said evenly. "Are you glad to see her again? Has she realized she made a mistake when she broke off your engagement?"

"Rather pointed questions from someone who doesn't care what happens to me after September!"

"You know that's not true! You're the one who claims to be easily hurt by women! I just wondered if you were setting yourself up for another fall!" Lacey snapped.

"Kind of you to be concerned," he drawled, his hands tightening on her back. "But don't worry about Joanna. She and I understand each other. Or, at least, I understand her," he amended thoughtfully. "You and Jeremy seem to be getting on well together this evening. Doesn't it bother him knowing you spent the day with me? Does he realize you didn't return immediately to your cottage last night?"

Lacey flushed. "Jeremy and I understand each other, too," she shot back with an acid sweetness.

"Meaning he doesn't hold last night against you?"

"He doesn't know anything about last night! Except that I didn't return to the cottage for a while!"

"Honey, by now most of the people in this room know about last night," Holt informed her with a certain satisfaction.

"What!" Lacey's shock was genuine. Her wide eyes and faintly parted lips testified to that. "How could they? I mean, I certainly never told..."

"I was seen coming back from your cottage," he explained in a kindlier tone. Something in his face softened at the evidence of her distress. "It's okay, honey. No one cares. If anything they're quite happy for us! Everyone loves a romance. But it does increase the speculation now that Joanna has arrived on the scene. It won't be long before she knows about us, if she doesn't already.''

"My God! This is as bad as Iowa!"

"Does that bother you?"

"I have no desire to be embarrassed!" she responded furiously.

"You have to learn to handle this kind of situation," he told her deliberately.

"Just as I have to learn to handle one-night stands? How dare you, Holt Randolph! Go back to your ex-fiancée! I'll bet she's an old hand at dealing with such situations. Just don't come whining to me when she decides she's through playing with you for the summer!"

Without waiting for his reaction, Lacey whirled out of his arms and strode back across the floor toward the small table. Jeremy hadn't returned yet with his unwilling partner. Lacey retrieved her small purse and walked firmly toward the door, ignoring the interested glances which followed her progress.

She was almost there when Jeremy appeared magically at her side.

"I'll see you back to the cottage," he said simply, taking her arm with unexpected forcefulness. "This kind of exit always looks better when it's done with the assistance of a partner."

"Thanks, but that's not necessary," Lacey began seethingly, at a loss to fully explain her burst of temper. Why had she allowed that woman to upset her so? Was she really so concerned about Holt getting hurt by his ex-fiancée?

"I insist," Jeremy chuckled. "Besides, you're not the only one escaping."

"She got to you, is that it?" Lacey found herself smiling.

"She was furious at being foisted off on me and didn't hesitate to let me know it. The lady has the manners of a she-cat!" Jeremy growled as he led Lacey out into the cool night air.

"Funny, she looked all honey and cream when she was dancing with Holt!"

"A word of warning, pal, she's aware of you...."

"I know that." Lacey shrugged indifferently.

"No, I mean she's aware of your role in Holt's life right now."

"I don't have a particular role, dammit!"

"Whatever you say, Lacey," he soothed. "I'm just trying to warn you. I think she's come back to the island for Holt and she's not going to let anything stand in her way."

"I don't intend to try! If Holt wants to resume the engagement, that's his business!" Lacey lifted her chin proudly. "I have my own plans for the future!"

"I believe you!" he asserted quickly as they reached her cottage doorstep.

Lacey took pity on him. "I'm sorry, Jeremy, I don't know why I'm acting like this! Come on in and have a nightcap. It's the least I can do to thank you for trying to rescue me this evening!"

"Thanks, I accept," he said at once, dark eyes lightening.

He left half an hour later, cheerfully accepting her casual, friendly farewell kiss at her door. She stood watching as he set off for his own cottage in the distance, thinking that he was really a very nice man, and then she walked slowly back into the house and shut the door.

She stood quietly for a moment, wondering what Holt was doing with his ex-fiancée and then, disgustedly, told herself not to worry about it. She collected the glasses from the coffee table and walked into the kitchen.

The knock on her door caught her just as she finished rinsing out the snifter Jeremy had used. Going very still with the intuitive knowledge of who it must be, Lacey thought of her alternatives.

Then, as if mesmerized by an inescapable doom, she trailed across the living room and opened the door.

"Don't tell me you weren't expecting me," Holt commanded with mocking dryness. He lounged in her doorway, a bottle of cognac in one hand.

"I wasn't," she lied. "What are you doing here, Holt?"

He straightened and stepped past her into the room. "That's easy, I came to take Todd's place." He threw himself down on the sofa and cocked her a meaningful glance. "Took you long enough to throw him out. Five more minutes and I might have lost my temper and done something rash."

"Nonsense," Lacey flung back tersely as she shut the door and crossed the room to sit across from him in the old, overstuffed chair by the fireplace. "You don't believe in doing rash things, remember? You're too concerned with the entire future!"

"*Our* entire future," he retorted. "Got a couple of glasses?"

"I just had a nightcap, thanks."

"Have another. I want to talk to you."

She eyed him, trying to judge his mood and then, without a word, rose to fetch two glasses from the kitchen.

Wordlessly they sipped the expensive cognac for a few moments, each involved with personal thoughts and then Lacey heard herself say, "How close did you come to marrying her?"

"Too close. Fortunately she realized at the last minute that I had no intention of being dragged off this island. She had visions of getting me back into the hotel business, I think. Saw herself living a jet-set life-style.''

"Like me?" she couldn't help saying.

"No, not quite." He smiled. "She wanted a man to pay her way."

"You."

"Yes."

"Did you love her?" Lacey asked remotely.

He shrugged. "I was attracted to her. She came along shortly after I'd made the decision to stay here and bring the inn back in style. I think I had some vague idea of believing the place needed a beautiful hostess. The engagement didn't last long. She realized I was serious about the inn and she promptly became serious about someone else."

"Were you…badly hurt?"

"Is that sympathy I hear?"

"Just a question," she said quietly.

"No, I wasn't badly hurt. My main emotion at the time was one of relief."

Lacey nodded understandingly. "That's how I felt after Roger finally told me he wanted a divorce."

"Speaking of Roger…"

Holt's words were cut off by the ringing of the telephone. Lacey glanced at it in disgust. "Yes, speaking of Roger," she muttered, letting the phone ring again.

"That's him?" One tawny brow lifted inquiringly.

"Probably." The phone rang again. Lacey didn't move.

"Want me to answer it?" Holt offered, holding her eyes.

A slow smile curved her mouth as she considered that. "You're wicked to tempt me like this." The thought of Roger's face when he heard a man answering the phone in Lacey's cottage at this hour of the night was irresistible.

Without waiting for a definite affirmative, Holt reached across and lifted the receiver from the cradle.

"Yes?" he drawled politely, his eyes still on Lacey's. "No, you don't have the wrong number. This is the phone in Lacey's cottage."

There was a pause and a rather menacing mischief lit the silvery gaze. "I'm afraid that's not possible. Lacey's busy at the moment. Take my word for it. Who am I? I'm the one who's keeping her busy, naturally."

The response to that was audible as a muffled shout to Lacey. Roger sounded as if he had exploded.

"No, I'm not going to let you speak to her," Holt said calmly into the phone. "I never let strange men speak to my fiancée. Especially at this hour of the night!'' Very gently he replaced the telephone and lifted challenging eyes to meet Lacey's.

She stared at him, not knowing whether to be shocked or incredibly amused. For an instant she hovered on the brink and then she grinned. ''A little drastic, but effective. I would have given a fortune to see his face!''

''You're not angry?'' he queried cautiously, lifting his cognac glass.

''I'll have to do some explaining in the morning, I suppose. He'll be on the phone to my parents soon as it's light back there. I expect I'll be hearing from them before breakfast!''

''But you can talk your way out of it?'' he persisted.

She lifted one shoulder dismissingly. ''I'll tell them the facts. They can deal with them as they wish. I've already told mom I have no interest in Roger. She should have known better than to give my number out to him.''

''You seem very calm about having to explain your 'fiancé,' '' Holt murmured, staring down into his glass as if fascinated by the amber liquid.

''There's not much to explain.'' She smiled, watching the play of lamplight on his light brown hair. Holt was still wearing the jacket and tie he'd had on earlier in the lounge. The sight of him sitting on her sofa pleased her for some strange reason.

She wondered where Joanna Davis was at that moment.

"Since the idea doesn't seem to bother you," he began slowly, "I wonder if you would mind returning the favor...."

"Sorry, I seem to have lost the thread of the conversation...." Lacey said very carefully.

He looked up, his hazel eyes suddenly very serious. "Isn't it clear? I'm asking you to help me get rid of Joanna."

She stared at him, her thoughts sliding abruptly into chaos. "What are you talking about?" she got out in a faint whisper of apprehension.

"I want to tell Joanna that you and I are engaged. I want to make it clear that I have no interest in her."

"You don't need me to help you do that," Lacey breathed tautly, her drink forgotten in her hand.

"No," he agreed. "But it would sure as hell simplify things."

It dawned on her that Holt hadn't been completely honest in his explanation of Joanna Davis. "You *are* afraid of being hurt by her, aren't you? You're not nearly so casual as you appear about her coming back into your life!"

He glanced away. "She's a very persistent woman...."

"Meaning you might find yourself back under her spell before you realize what's going on?"

"I'm not in love with her!" He got to his feet as if in irritation and walked across to lean against the mantel of the empty fireplace.

"But you're still attracted to her. You're worried she could play on the attraction, aren't you?" Lacey said perceptively, eyeing him closely.

"You're the only woman I want, Lacey," he told her quietly, still staring into the darkened hearth.

She caught her breath, unable to deny the small thrill his words brought. Slowly she rose to stand in front of him. "You think I can make you forget her?" she whispered softly.

He lifted his head to meet her gentle gaze. "Yes."

Her heart filled to overflowing with an emotion she didn't want to name. She only knew she didn't want Holt to be humiliated again by the woman who had gone off once before with another man. Lacey was astounded by her sense of protectiveness. Nor could she deny the sheer, feminine pleasure it would give her to spike the other woman's guns. Holt had done her a favor in getting the pesky Roger off her back tonight. Why shouldn't she return it? He didn't deserve to be hurt again by Joanna Davis.

"If you think it will make life easier for you, go ahead and tell her that you and I are going to be married," she invited softly.

His fingers clenched almost white on the mantel and then he relaxed, smiling with a flash of genuine amusement. "You don't mind?"

"If anyone else gets wind of it, we'll just say there's been a misunderstanding," Lacey said with an indifference she was far from feeling.

He stepped away from the mantel and threw a possessively affectionate arm around her shoulders. "Come on, fiancée, let's go for a walk. I feel the need of a little exercise."

"At midnight!" she exclaimed, taken aback by his sudden cheerfulness.

"It's either that or I shall probably try to make love to you, and I honestly didn't come here tonight for that purpose!" He grabbed the shawl she had thrown across the back of the sofa earlier and settled it around her shoulders.

"Such restraint," she mocked, hiding her abrupt and fierce desire to have him do exactly that. What was the matter with her this evening?

"I know," he groaned, leading her down the path to the small bay in front of the inn. "But look on the bright side. My restraint's been known to slip before!"

"Is that a threat?" she demanded, laughing up at him. In the moonlight her eyes sparkled, taunting him, at once wary and provoking.

He drew her to a halt on the shadowy lawn. In the background the sound of the band in the lounge could be heard. But the only things Lacey was conscious of were the lambent flames in Holt's eyes and the feel of his arms as he pulled her close in the moonlight.

"Sweetheart, don't tempt me unless you're prepared to take the consequences. I've been aching for you all day. And then, tonight, I had to listen to you talking to your ex-husband, watch you dancing with Todd. It's been a rough day!"

Lacey looked up at him, blue-green eyes shadowed as she acknowledged the extent of her own longing. She thought of the black-haired woman from Holt's past, remembered the passion of the previous evening, and then recalled her pleasure in the day she had spent with him. She wanted this man and he wanted her. Once again she had no wish to consider the future. It lay out there, waiting for her. She would get to it soon enough when the summer ended. Weren't the feelings of the moment exactly what she was seeking, anyway?

Then she remembered Holt's anger from the night before and the glow faded from her eyes. She tried to gently free herself.

"What's wrong, honey?"

"I want you, Holt, but you made it clear last night that it will never work. I can't make the kind of promises you want...." she whispered brokenly.

"Are you sure of that, little Lacey?" he asked beguilingly. He bent to push aside the sweep of auburn hair and drop a warm, lingering kiss just below her ear. "Are you positive you can't make the kind of promises I want?"

"Holt, we've been through this," she protested, trembling as his hands kneaded the length of her spine and found the curve of her hips. Eyes shut against the need he was arousing in her, Lacey stood very still in his embrace.

"If you can't make the promises, do you think you could pretend?" he coaxed, urging her body tightly against his thighs, leaving her in no doubt of his growing desire.

"Pre-pretend?"

"I want you so much and you've admitted you want me. Why don't we both forget about the future tonight and pretend we really are engaged."

"Another one-night stand?" she asked sadly.

"No, we've already had that," he rasped huskily, finding the line of her throat with his lips. "After the second night I think we can classify it as an affair."

"And will there be a third night?"

"Yes."

"Holt, do you realize what you're saying?" she pleaded as common sense once more fled beneath his touch.

"That I'm surrendering? That, like it or not, I'm agreeing to do things your way? I realize it. I knew after I'd taken you back to the cottage last night that I'd wind up on my knees. I've spent the day coming to terms with that fact. I'd only hoped I could hold out a little longer, give you a little more time to understand.... But I can't resist you, sweetheart. I'll take what I can get.''

Wordlessly he took her hand and started toward the Victorian home at the far end of the lodge.

# Nine

Why was it so difficult to accept this man's surrender? Lacey's emotions warred within her as Holt led her up the steps and across the glassed-in porch. She felt his hand trembling ever so slightly as he halted to open the front door and she couldn't quite meet his eyes as she stepped over the threshold.

Holt closed the door and then, one hand on her shoulder, he turned her slowly around to face him. He scanned her still features as if searching for evidence of the battle raging within her. But he couldn't even begin to guess how shaken she was, Lacey told herself. Who could have predicted that at the very moment she was being handed what she wanted, a passionate relationship with no strings attached, something within her was beginning to question the goal.

"What's the matter, honey?" he asked half humorously, half passionately. "Are you afraid I'm going to throw you out of my bed again this evening?"

"Are you?" she asked starkly, wondering if, out of disgust with himself, he wouldn't do exactly that.

"Oh, Lacey." He groaned, wrapping her close, his face in her hair. "I'd never have the strength to do it again. As soon as I'd taken you home last night I regretted it. Don't worry, honey, I've accepted my fate!"

Lacey winced at the words, hearing the quiet decision behind them. The protective instincts she had experienced earlier when he'd more or less asked her help in fending off Joanna surged to the for.

"Holt, if this isn't what you want..." she mumbled earnestly into his shoulder and instantly felt his grasp tighten.

"It's what I want. And it's what you want, isn't it?"

"I...I think so...." She was upset with the halting confession and wished it could have been retracted.

"You *think* so!" he echoed with a hint of incredulity. Both hands moving to frame her face, he held her a little away from him and stared down at her. "Don't you know for sure? Have you changed your mind about wanting me after all? So soon?"

"No, oh no, Holt!" Swiftly her fingers came up, settling urgently on his shoulders. "I want you. It's just that everything's happening so quickly. And there's Joanna...." she trailed off weakly.

"Forget Joanna. She had nothing to do with this decision of mine tonight. But I do appreciate your help in getting rid of her. You meant it, didn't you, Lacey? You'll let me tell her we're engaged?"

Glad to be able to give even so small a thing in the face of his far greater surrender, Lacey nodded quickly. "Tell her whatever you want, Holt."

He caught his breath and once again she felt the fine trembling in his hands. "Then tonight we'll pretend we really are going to be married," he murmured. "And in the morning we'll forget the game."

She felt his breath lightly stir her hair as he kissed her with exquisite delicacy on the temple. He held aside the red-brown mass and lowered his mouth to the tip of her ear. Every movement was incredibly slow, infinitely tantalizing.

Slowly, as if she were a present which must be unwrapped with utmost care, Holt continued the delicious exploration. He planted tiny, stinging little kisses down the line of her throat to the curve of her shoulder and groaned as he felt her begin to melt against him.

Lacey's hands moved across his chest, sliding under the fabric of his jacket and seeking the warmth of his body. She inhaled the clean, masculine scent of him and unconsciously leaned her smaller weight more fully against his strength.

He stroked her with long, sensual movements that went from her head to her hips, leaving her body aching with the need he seemed able to arouse in her so easily. She arched in languid, luxurious response, closing her eyes and leaning her head against his shoulder.

"You feel as if you were made for me," he whispered deeply. "You respond so perfectly and you make me respond so easily. I only have to look at you to want you."

She stirred as he shaped the curve of her derriere, scooping her tightly against his lower body so that she was made aware of his desire. "You're not thinking about Joanna?" she tried to say lightly, teasingly. But she wasn't at all sure she'd buried the seriousness of the question in her voice.

She felt him smile against the skin of her shoulder. "I can only think about you, sweetheart. What about Roger Wesley? Are you thinking about him?"

She opened the collar of his shirt and dropped a butterfly kiss at the base of his throat. "Don't be ridiculous. Roger comes under the category of nuisance. I'm afraid I took an unholy pleasure in letting you tell him we were engaged."

"Don't worry about it. He deserved it," Holt assured her smoothly.

"Still, it was a lie." - She sighed hesitantly, frowning slightly as she considered what her family would go through in the morning when Roger delivered his bombshell.

"To make a lie seem convincing, you have to act as if you believe it yourself," Holt advised, sweeping her up into his arms with sudden determination. "I think we should get in some practice."

Lacey wondered at the resolve in his voice and then she forgot about the lie and what her family would think as he carried her into the shadowy bedroom with its huge, four-poster bed. As he set her on her feet, she forgot about everything in the world except Holt Randolph.

"I need you so much, Holt," she breathed. "I..." She stumbled over the next word, realizing with a distant sense of shock that she had been on the edge of proclaiming her love. But that was impossible! They weren't in love. They shared a passion and that was all!

"You what, sweetheart?" he murmured encouragingly, slipping the white painter's shirt off and letting it drop to the floor. He found her unconfined breasts and wove delicate patterns on the tips to bring them to taut fullness.

"Nothing," she got out shakily. "I...I can't seem to think very straight at the moment...."

"Neither can I," he admitted huskily, sliding his hands reluctantly from her breasts down to her stomach, to find the fastening of her skirt. "You're like a drug in my veins."

He buried his face in her throat as he undid her skirt. In another moment or two she stood naked, her body gleaming softly in the dim light of a bedside lamp.

"Undress me," he ordered thickly, straining her to him. "I want to feel you touch me."

Lacey needed no further encouragement. With hands made awkward by passion she slowly removed his clothes. It took awhile and he didn't help her. Instead he stood still and let her take her time. It was as if he were luxuriating in the small service.

At last she undid the buckle of his belt, unzipped his slacks, and slid her hands inside the waistband. Slowly she pushed them over his strong thighs, going down on one knee to ease them off entirely.

Her hands circled his hair-roughened calves as she knelt, naked, in front of him, and she lifted her face in the pale light.

"You shouldn't be kneeling at my feet," he got out, his tone hoarse with desire. "I should be kneeling at yours!" But when she moved without a word to press hot, pleading kisses against his thighs his hands twisted themselves imperatively in her hair. "Lacey, my sweet Lacey!"

She sank her fingers into the muscled length of him and slowly straightened, covering the length of his body with increasingly passionate caresses. Across the flatness of his stomach, over the male nipples, up to the curve of his shoulder. Her hands moved on his back, kneading, pressing, dancing on his skin.

"You've got me half out of my mind!" he growled when she stood at last in front of him again.

She thrilled to the primitive timbre of his voice glorying in the knowledge that she was capable of arousing him. Until she had met Holt she had never dreamed a man could give himself to a woman even as he took her completely. It seemed to be a contradiction but the ultimate result was exciting beyond anything she had ever known.

"Oh." She sighed as he gently assumed control of the lovemaking, lifting her off her feet and sliding her into bed. "Oh, Holt, I never thought it would be like this...."

The rest of the small confession was cut off as he came down beside her, finding her curving body with hands that beseeched and beguiled.

Under the impact of his touch, Lacey gave herself up to him completely, making no secret of her need, just as he made no secret of his. For long, endless moments they coaxed delighted responses from each other.

Holt smoothed her skin with anticipation and deliberate seductiveness until Lacey was a trembling, twisting creature of passion, longing only to find the fulfillment she had known once before with him. He seemed to delight in the increasing fervor of her demands as if his greatest pleasure lay in first invoking them and then satisfying them.

When she grew impatient, pulling him to her with compelling fingers, he held back a while longer. Her head moved restlessly in protest on the pillow.

"Please, Holt. Please love me!"

"Love you?"

She hadn't been aware of her words until he repeated them huskily and by then she was beyond a semantics argument. Instead she arched her lower body invitingly against him, pleading silently for the culmination of passion.

Eventually, as if intent on pushing her to the limits of her own desire, Holt moved, settling on his back and pulling her down on top of him. Lacey gasped aloud at the unexpected position and then surrendered entirely to the thrill of setting the rhythm of their desire.

Her nails bit into his shoulders as she enveloped him with her heat and the desire he had elicited in her. Lacey lost all track of time, her world focused only around the two of them.

And then Holt shifted again; the hands which had been gently raking her hips suddenly seized her waist and tossed her lightly down on the bed. "You're mine, Lacey," he rasped as he took erotic command of her body. "You've given yourself to me and this time there's no mistake...."

She didn't understand the meaning of his words so she ignored them, crying out with pleasure as he mastered her swimming senses. In that moment she was his and the completeness of the surrender didn't bother her at all. She wanted to belong totally to this man and make him belong just as totally to her. It was all that mattered.

Holt's driving, graceful power swept them both into the irresistible tide of desire. Lacey felt the shock of electricity flowing through her, seething into a tight mass in her nether regions. Desperately she clung, heedless of the fine red lines her nails were drawing on Holt's bronzed back.

And then at last they found the ultimate release together, holding each other in an unshakable clasp as it rocked them.

The blinding realization came upon Holt even before the final tremors had washed through her system. She shut her eyes against the knowledge, told herself it was a temporary by-product of satisfied physical need. But when she opened them to stare blankly at the ceiling, the truth of what had happened was still there, taunting her, frightening her. She was in love with Holt.

She turned her head slightly to look at him wonderingly. He lay beside her, his legs still twined with hers, the picture of satiated masculinity. He obviously had no comprehension of what had happened to her.

He regarded her with lazy satisfaction as she stared at him. "Don't look so anxious." He chuckled deeply. "You're not going anywhere. I'm not about to make the mistake I did last night!"

He pulled her head against his perspiration-dampened chest, idly stroking his fingers through her tangled hair. "I couldn't let you go again," he whispered simply.

Obediently, Lacey let him hold her close for a few minutes, sensing his need for the quiet communion. The silence between them was fine with her. She was almost too stunned to speak!

She had achieved her goal. She had what she thought she wanted and now, too late, she discovered it wasn't what she craved, after all.

In painful realization of the full extent of her stupidity, Lacey shut her eyes to keep back the hint of moisture. What was she going to do? How did she even begin to explain to Holt? The whole mess, she found herself thinking with a tinge of anger, was his fault, anyway!

If it hadn't been for him she would still be blissfully planning a sparkling future. Instead she had been handed a slice of that future and found it didn't work.

The passion which had taken her by storm had its roots in love. A love beyond anything she had ever known. She didn't want a finite encounter with this man which would end in September. She wanted him for the rest of her life. She wanted marriage.

Even as she thought of the word, Lacey winced inwardly. Marriage was the one thing Holt hadn't offered! An indefinite affair based on mutual desire, yes. But not marriage based on old-fashioned love. Darkly she remembered his words when she had foolishly asked him if he loved her a little. He'd told her she'd asked the wrong question. He'd admitted he wanted her indefinitely but he hadn't claimed to love her.

Suddenly, in the chaotic aftermath, Lacey knew one thing very clearly. She wanted Holt's love.

But the knowledge didn't pacify her, it alternately infuriated her and depressed her! This wasn't what she'd planned for the past two years!

Beside her, Holt stirred, his fingers trailing lightly down her arm. "What are you thinking, honey? You're very quiet lying there...."

"Nothing," she lied, unable to even begin to talk

about it. "I...I wasn't thinking of anything in particular...."

"Liar," he murmured affectionately. "But it's all right. There will be plenty of time for talking in the morning."

They slept eventually, Lacey held tightly in Holt's embrace. She hadn't expected to be able to even doze given the turmoil of her mind, but the next thing she knew, sunlight was pouring in through the windows, illuminating the magnificent body of the man sprawled out beside her.

With a strange nervousness, Lacey edged carefully out of bed, finding her clothes on the floor and heading for the bath. She was a bundle of agitation and chaotic thoughts, she realized dimly as she stepped beneath the hot water in the shower. She was in the midst of an emotional crisis!

What was the matter with her? In the light of a new day she should be able to put aside the strange illusions of the night. They had been the product of desire, she told herself again and again. Love was not a factor in the equation which was her future. Passion, excitement, anticipation, and adventure. Those were the factors she had decided to work with. That was what had been missing back in Iowa. Wasn't it?

With a groan she wondered if what had really been missing in Iowa was love.

Every iota of rational sense told her to fight the

sensation. But how did you fight this abiding emotion for another human being? With one breath she told herself she couldn't possibly be in love with Holt. And with the next she knew it so firmly there didn't seem to be any defense against the knowledge. It was like trying to hide from herself.

All right, she instructed herself firmly as she stood beneath the hot spray, for the sake of argument, suppose you are in love. What happens next? Holt isn't in love with you....

But he wants me, she thought at once. He wants me and he needs me. Perhaps he is in love and doesn't recognize it. Perhaps Joanna Davis had really burned him with her callous treatment.

"Is this a private party or can anyone join?"

Lacey flicked open her eyes, swinging around to face Holt as he climbed into the shower beside her. She eyed him nervously but he seemed oblivious of her uncertain mood.

"You look cute in the mornings," he announced, stooping slightly to kiss the tip of her nose. "Cute and sexy."

"Good morning, Holt," she managed, not knowing what else to say. She wanted to fling her arms around him and confess her love. And in the next second she wanted to hit out at him for playing havoc with her future. She swung violently from one extreme to the other and the insanity of the alternating emotions was unnerving.

"Is that the best you can do?" he mocked fondly, sliding her wet body into his arms and kissing her with lingering warmth. "Ummm. You taste good in the mornings, too." He lifted his head and then carried her wrist to his mouth where he planted another soft caress. She felt his tongue deliberately tasting her skin and pulled her hand away.

As soon as she'd made the rather abrupt maneuver, she regretted it. He was bound to notice her wary, almost hostile attitude and question it. But when she shot him a swift glance out of the corner of her eye she realized he hadn't paid her small action any attention. Instead, he was cheerfully soaping himself and chatting about the day ahead.

"How would you like to take another trip out on the boat this afternoon, Lacey? Maybe to that cove where we went last time. I think I can spare a couple of hours. We could take dinner with us and picnic. We'd be back in time for the evening brandy hour. Sound good?"

"Er...yes, I suppose so," she mumbled, scrubbing her face vigorously with a washcloth. Anything to keep from having to look directly at him.

"It's going to be a great summer, sweetheart," he went on easily. "I decided last night I'm just not going to think about the future. We'll take what comes and enjoy it while we can, right?"

Lacey, who suddenly couldn't think of anything else except the new, uncharted future she faced nearly choked. Muttering something which she hoped sounded vaguely suitable, she hurried through her washing, anxious to escape the close confines of the shower.

But breakfast was worse. To her horror she burned the toast, spilled the orange juice, made lousy coffee, and generally came apart at the seams.

"Funny," Holt said teasingly when she almost flung the overcooked eggs in front of him. "I thought any woman who came from Iowa could cook. Another case of stereotyping, I guess."

"I *can* cook!" she retorted vehemently, throwing herself into the seat across from him. "I'm just not used to your kitchen!"

"I understand," he soothed in that tone of voice men always use when they're trying to placate women but secretly find them amusing. "Well, if things don't improve tomorrow morning we can always eat up at the lodge."

"I haven't said I'll move in with you, Holt!" she gasped, appalled by his assumption.

"My mistake," he allowed smoothly. "You're in charge of this relationship. We'll do things the way you want."

That reply didn't please her one bit better than the first comment. Seethingly, Lacey tried to get through the meal, letting Holt do most of the talking. Her mind skipped back and forth from one emotional topic to the next as she tried desperately to figure out what she was going to do with her life.

She nearly dropped a cup when she started to clear the table. Holt was helping her, and he looked up in mild concern as she caught the descending piece of china shortly before it struck the floor.

"Good catch," he approved condescendingly.

Lacey nearly hurled the offending cup at him, noting just in time the expensive name on the base. One didn't toss English bone china at the head of one's lover. Did one?

Holt didn't seem to be aware of his close call. He finished carrying his stack of dishes into the old-fashioned country kitchen, calling out to her casually as he disappeared. "I'm going to spend the morning in the office, if you need me. What are you going to do today?"

Lacey looked at the cup in her hand. "Go through an entire midlife crisis in one day," she muttered inaudibly.

"What?" he called.

"I don't know yet!" she nearly shouted, barely regaining control of her voice before it disintegrated into a sob.

He reappeared in the kitchen doorway, smiling placidly. "How about meeting me for lunch in the main dining room?" He glanced at his watch. "That will give you plenty of time for a nice swim before lunch and maybe a little meditation, too. I'm going to have to forgo my run this morning. We're a little late...."

"Yes, yes, that will be fine," she agreed hurriedly.

"Excellent." He nodded, looking totally satisfied with life. "I'll meet you at noon at the entrance to the dining room."

Lacey bit back in argument. What could she say?

He waved good-bye to her a short time later at the junction of the path which led to her cottage, striding off to work with such good-natured enthusiasm that Lacey could have screamed. How dare he act as if everything in life was perfectly fine? Didn't he realize she was about to come unglued?

The phone was ringing authoritatively as she walked back into her cottage. Lacey glared at it, intuition and logic dictating who was on the other end. She seriously considered not answering it. She wasn't in the mood to talk to anyone, least of all her family from Iowa. She had a severe dilemma on her hands. Couldn't anyone comprehend that this morning?

Incredibly annoyed at the world's lack of sensitivity to her, Lacey lifted the receiver in disgust. "Hello, mother," she said without waiting for the caller to identify herself.

"Lacey! Lacey, what's going on out there? We just had a call from your husband...!"

"My ex-husband."

"Roger—" Martha Seldon forged on "—says there was a man answering your phone last night at a very late hour. A man claiming to be engaged to you!"

"Roger has good ears," Lacey observed dryly.

"Well?"

"Well, what?" She knew she was being deliberately obtuse and couldn't help it.

"Well, is it true?" Mrs. Seldon demanded in exasperation.

"Quite true. And now, if you don't mind, I've got other things to do this morning...."

"Lacey! Don't you dare hang up this phone. I want to know what's happening out there!"

"I've gotten myself engaged. Don't worry, Mom, you're going to love him."

Lacey hung up the phone with great care and quickly grabbed her swimsuit before her mother had a chance to redial.

As she walked past George in the lobby on her way to the indoor pool she waved airily. "Good morning, George. I'll be in the pool room. But for the record, I'm not taking any more telephone calls from Iowa this morning, understood?"

"Perfectly, Miss Seldon," George murmured, one gray brow arched with unspoken query.

Lacey didn't bother to answer the silent question. She had too many of her own to work on at the moment.

# *Ten*

The pool room was empty at this early hour. Lacey changed quickly into the maillot and began doing what she seldom did in a pool. Laps. A lot of them.

It didn't take any great psychological insight to realize she was trying to work out her frustrations in a physical manner, she decided vengefully as she surfaced at the shallow end and caught her breath.

But the activity only seemed to bring the facts into even harsher perspective. No matter what kind of logic she used, the only thing which really mattered any more was Holt Randolph. And Holt was content with an affair.

Tossing her head angrily to shake off water as she emerged from the pool, Lacey reached for a towel. What had happened last night to put her into this crisis?

It had to do with Holt's surrender. She gritted her teeth and marched toward the changing rooms to slip back into a pair of jeans and a breezy, oversized bush shirt. Up until last night Holt had always been pushing for a commitment. Lacey was shocked at herself to realize how much that had meant. She had repeatedly told him and herself that it wasn't what she wanted, but as long as he kept demanding it, some part of her had subconsciously relaxed and felt free to go into an affair.

Last night Holt had taken her on her own terms and Lacey had discovered she didn't like her own terms. Now he seemed satisfied with what Lacey claimed to want.

Trailing dismally out of the pool room, she dropped her wet swimsuit off at the cottage and set out on a brisk walk along the tree-lined shore. Perhaps a little exercise in the fresh air would help. Heaven knew she needed something to clear her head!

But her thoughts continued to chase each other relentlessly. She wanted Holt but she wanted him on the terms he had originally set. No, she wanted more. She wanted marriage. But, she realized with a pang, she was the one who was now desperate enough to take him on just about any basis.

What about her bright exciting future? Was she simply going to forget what she had planned for so long? She tried to remind herself of how much the excitement of an unknown, adventuresome future had drawn her. And all she could think about was the excitement and passion she had found in Holt's arms.

Was she caught up in her own snare? Was she mistaking physical attraction for love?

Lacey swung around at the end of the shoreline path and headed back toward the cottage. No, she knew this was different. In spite of the restrictions of her life, she had learned a few things in her time, enough to distinguish between lust and love. The feelings she had for Holt went far beyond the physical. She wanted to protect him from Joanna, she enjoyed the most casual of conversations with him, she even liked arguing with him. The list was endless. She was in love.

Still her mind whirled with the unexpected shock she had received last night. The realization that she desperately missed his demand for a commitment in their relationship, the dismay she had experienced over having had her future plans thrown into chaos, the bitter knowledge that she had found herself unsuited to the life-style she thought she'd wanted. All of these ricocheted back and forth in her head like rifle shots.

And what did a woman do when a man threw her into a crisis of this magnitude while surrendering his demands at the same time? It didn't even leave her anyone to argue with over the matter! Only herself. Yesterday morning, at least, she'd had the luxury of being furious with him.

Back at the cottage, Lacey stalked briefly around the living room, restlessly trying to marshal her thoughts. It wouldn't be long before she was due to meet Holt for lunch. What would she say? How could she possibly explain her nervousness?

Perhaps she'd been taking the wrong approach in trying to settle her emotions physically. With the air of one choosing a last resort, Lacey walked out into the grassy area behind the cottage. It was fairly private out here, and although it wasn't dawn, she distinctly felt the need to try to compose herself.

Deliberately she settled into her meditation position, mentally charging her high-strung nerves to relax even as she eased her limbs into a quiet, composed state.

This was what she should have done in the first place she thought fleetingly as the world seemed to calm down around her. She closed her eyes, her hands slightly curled as they rested on her folded knees.

For long moments she didn't try to think at all, merely letting the soft island breeze ruffle her hair and catch lightly at her rakish-looking shirt. The warm sun beat down on her and she pictured herself absorbing the heat.

She let her mind run free for a time and then gradually, steadily, she began to seek a focus for her thoughts. She found it in her feelings for Holt.

Carefully, without trying to force any conclusions, she let her mind settle in place. She had come out West seeking answers. Back in Iowa it had been easy to think those answers lay in a lifestyle totally alien to what she had tolerated for so long.

But the answers weren't to be found in a lifestyle such as she had sought. She knew that now. She wasn't really seeking a different way of living; she had come looking for what had been missing in her previous life. She had found it with Holt, and because she hadn't been expecting to discover something so important in a man of his nature, she'd almost overlooked it.

Slowly the tension eased out of her, leaving her calm and clear-headed at last. The sense of being totally unnerved faded to be replaced by a certainty which people out West labeled midwestern stubbornness. She knew what she wanted now. It only remained to be seen if Holt wanted the same thing.

Lacey was unaware of time passing. Eyes closed, she let her senses drift, inhaling the sent of the woods and grass, aware of the hard ground beneath her, alert to the small sounds of birds in the trees.

At last, sensing a change in the atmosphere around her, Lacey slowly opened her eyes. Holt was crouched in front of her, an incredibly gentle smile in his eyes. Beside him rested a small basket.

"Crisis over?" he asked softly.

She stared at him. "I love you, Holt."

"I know that," he murmured, settling more firmly into a cross-legged sitting position opposite her. "Hungry? When you didn't show up for lunch I decided to come looking...."

"What do you mean, you know it!" She gasped, ignoring the offer of food.

He looked up from his investigation of the contents of the basket, a whimsical twist to his lips. "I knew it as soon as I had you in my bed, although I was madder than hell when you didn't recognize it yourself. Small-town midwestern librarians like you aren't very good at concealing such things when you're lying in a man's arms. You gave yourself to me. Completely. Women intent on not getting totally involved with a man don't surrender in bed like that. Nor do they fret about him being hurt by ex-fiancées...."

"You're an expert on the subject?" she demanded a little acidly. Some of her initial calm was disappearing in the fact of his bland acceptance of her love.

"I keep telling you, I've been where you thought you wanted to go. I know that what we have is what really counts," he said simply as he removed a chilled bottle of wine from the basket and began to uncork it.

Lacey drew a deep breath and took the plunge. "Holt, stop messing around with that bottle of wine and listen to me. I said I love you. Where I come from, barring complications, that means marriage," she said starkly.

He appeared to consider this carefully, his hands resting on the neck of the wine bottle. "What sort of complications might get in the way back where you come from?"

"If you...if you didn't love me, too...."

He went back to work on the cork. "Then there aren't any complications, are there? Of course I love you, you little idiot. I've loved you from the first moment I saw you!"

"Holt!"

Lacey yanked the still unopened bottle of wine out of his hands and set it firmly in the basket. Then she thew herself into his arms. Her eyes were gleaming as she raised them to meet his. "Do you mean that?" she breathed, clinging fiercely to his neck. "You love me?"

He held her tightly to him and smoothed her hair back from her anxious face. "I love you," he whispered, silvery eyes warm and compelling. "I intended to marry you just as soon as I could get you to stop thinking about a crazy future full of reckless affairs and shallow, meaningless adventures. Just ask your mother if you don't believe me," he added with a sudden hint of amusement.

"My mother!"

"Umm. Somebody had to talk to her this morning. Poor George was going crazy trying to explain that you weren't taking any calls from Iowa!"

"Oh, my God!" Lacey stared up at him, struck by the thought of her mother and Holt discussing the subject.

"Don't worry, she's so damn grateful to me for saving you from heaven knows what that I'm practically a member of the family in her eyes. Roger, you'll be happy to know, has now been relegated to the status of interfering turkey."

"My mother s a very practical woman." Lacey groaned ruefully. "Roger was a viable alternative just as long as he was the *only* alternative. As soon as something better appeared on the scene, his fate was sealed."

"So you do consider me a viable alternative?" he pressed, the humor going out of his voice as his grip on her tightened. "You're sure this is what you want, Lacey? I couldn't bear it if something changed your mind in the future. I couldn't let you go...."

"I'm sure," she whispered, her eyes serene and confident. "Last night when you said you were giving up and that you were going to do things my way, I realized I didn't want the relationship on those terms. With you I wanted a total commitment. When you no longer demanded that, it left my words ringing in my ears. Words about not wanting to tie myself down. I kept waiting for you to insist on permanency...."

"You had to realize that permanency was what you wanted, too," he said quietly. "I was so sure you were in love with me that I decided to take the chance last night of letting you find out for yourself."

"Did you deliberately dangle Joanna in front of me?" she demanded accusingly.

"Perhaps, a little," he admitted. "I was willing to try just about anything...."

Her eyes narrowed. "Where is Joanna, by the way? Did you give her the line about us being engaged?"

He hesitated and then confessed. "I gave her that line last night before I came to the cottage!"

Lacey was torn between indignation and laughter. "What would you have done this morning if I hadn't been so willing to come to your rescue?"

"Fortunately for me," he drawled smoothly, "I

wasn't left to face that particular problem. You were much too kindhearted to leave me defenseless in front of an old flame...."

"Were you defenseless? Holt, are you still afraid of being attracted to her? Because if you are..."

"Don't be ridiculous. My feelings for Joanna died a long time ago. Even at the time, what I felt for her is nothing compared to what I feel for you. I wasn't in love with Joanna. I am most definitely in love with you! Getting you to pretend to be engaged was just another attempt at tying you to me, I'm afraid. It had nothing to do with fending off Joanna!"

"She's still looking, isn't she?" Lacey said with abrupt intuition.

"Looking?"

"She's living the life-style I thought I wanted," she explained slowly. "She came back here searching for what she'd turned down the first time and it was no longer waiting."

"Joanna would only be genuinely interested in me again if she could persuade me to join her in the life-style she craves. She wants the money and the glamour and the superficiality. She doesn't want *me*. And even if she did, I'm no longer available." He grinned, brushing a possessive kiss across Lacey's lips. "I'm permanently spoken for by a stubborn little midwesterner who came a couple of thousand miles to claim me!''

Lacey sighed blissfully. ''Did you honestly fall in love with me at first sight?''

''How could I not? I'd been looking for you all my life,'' he said simply. ''You'll never know how terrified I was when I discovered you were intent on finding the fast life. I knew it would be all wrong for you, but I didn't know how to make you believe me.''

''You never tried saying anything about love and marriage.''

''The hell I didn't! Every time the subject came up, if you'll recall, you showed a disdainful lack of interest. Claimed marriage had nothing to offer you. When I tried to retreat to a demand for a long-term commitment, you still resisted. Do you wonder I didn't profess my love in the face of that sort of rejection?''

''And last night you were reduced to taking whatever you could get?''

''Not quite,'' he said evenly. ''I was so sure you loved me by then, I figured I could take the risk of pretending to surrender. I was hoping another night in my bed would show you that you wanted me on a permanent basis. I realized as soon as I awoke this morning that things were going along nicely....''

"Nicely!" Lacey flared. "That's a fine way of describing it! I was a nervous wreck all morning!"

"Don't you think I knew that? It gave me great hope," Holt told her with patent satisfaction. "I could see your little brain whirling with all the new realizations. Did you watch your whole future pass before your eyes?" he teased affectionately.

"I went through a severe emotional crisis this morning, Holt Randolph. I don't think it's very nice of you to tease me about it!"

"You're right. It's just that I'm so damned relieved!"

"What would you have done if I hadn't come to all my brilliant conclusions this morning?" she charged forcefully.

"I figured I had the rest of the summer to make you see the light. I would have let the affair continue under your terms until you finally realized what you really wanted," he told her sedately. And then a spark of vulnerability crept into his words. "I had no choice," he added honestly.

"No choice?" she questioned, sensing the meaning behind the small confession.

He shook his head, the expression in his eyes very naked. "I loved you too much to hold out against you, sweetheart. In a sense my surrender last night was genuine. I was willing to take whatever I could get. But I wanted so much more, and I was so sure you did, too...." He broke off, his mouth quirking in wry relief. "You gave me several bad moments over the past few days!"

"What do you think you were doing to me! You systematically shredded my whole perfectly planned future!" she shot back lightly, burying her face in his neck.

"Are you going to miss that future?" he whispered softly against her hair.

"No. I've replaced it with something I wanted a great deal more. It just took me awhile to realize it, that's all. After all, I didn't have your vast experience to draw on...."

"Thank God!" he muttered a little savagely. "I hate to think of what that life might have done to you, sweetheart. Like it or not, there's a lot of small-town U.S.A. in you. I was sure of that all along but that first night when you stood in my arms and asked me if I loved you a little, I realized how ill suited you were for the kind of life you thought you wanted!"

"You could have given me a little hint at that point about how you felt about me!" she mumbled into his shirt.

"I could have but I was afraid it would only delay your final acknowledgment of the truth. Besides," he added grimly, "I was a bit upset that night as I recall. Don't forget, I'd just found you kissing Todd in my swimming pool!"

"That meant nothing," she said hastily.

"I know. A little experiment. The first of many such experiments, if you had your way. I had to put a stop to it before it drove me insane!"

"It was a successful experiment, though." She chuckled unabashedly.

"What do you mean?" he asked warily.

"I knew as soon as Jeremy kissed me that his kisses weren't ever going to measure up to yours!"

"No more experiments, sweetheart, please!"

"No more. I promise. You're the only man I want, Holt. I do love you so much!"

"That," he murmured, "calls for a little celebration. I suggest we open that wine and drink to our future. If we don't, I'm liable to start making love to you right out here in public. Think what the guests would say!"

Holt finished opening the wine, poured it into two long-stemmed glasses, and handed her one. Silently they met each other's eyes over the crystal rims, and then they drank their toast to the future.

Lacey lowered her glass with a mischievous look. "You folks out West have a way of doing things with flare. Imagine drinking wine at this hour of the day out of crystal glasses while sitting on the grass!"

"We do our best." He shrugged modestly. "But personally, I'm looking forward to learning a lot of interesting midwestern customs in the future."

He became more serious for a moment. "I almost forgot. George gave me this to bring to you...."

He held the long white envelope out to her. The return address was clearly marked "Hawaii." He watched her take it, the anxious expression in his gaze not fully concealed.

Lacey glanced down at the envelope and then slowly tore it in two, dropping the pieces heedlessly beside her. "About my future career," she began softly.

"What about it, honey?" he whispered, some of the raw vulnerability back in his voice.

"Remember that boutique I talked about opening?" She smiled.

"I remember."

"Well, it strikes me this island could use that sort of shop. All these tourists hanging about during the summer and nothing to spend their money on except your food and drink!"

The lines at the edge of his mouth relaxed and he took the wineglass out of her hand, placing it beside his on the top of the basket. Slowly, with the satisfaction of a man who has his hands on the most important thing in life, he pulled her back into his arms. "Welcome home, Lacey my love," he said with infinite gentleness. "There was a time when I was terribly afraid you might not realize home was where you wanted to be."

"If you know how famous we midwestern librarians are for our common sense, you would never have doubted the final result for a moment!'' She lifted her face for his kiss, perfectly satisfied with the shape of the future.

\* \* \* \* \*

# SPECIAL EDITION

Stories of love and life, these powerful
novels are tales that you can identify with—
romances with "something special" added
in!

Fall in love with the stories of authors such
as **Nora Roberts, Diana Palmer, Ginna Gray**
and many more of your special favorites—as
well as wonderful new voices!

Special Edition brings you
entertainment for the heart!

SSE-GEN

# SILHOUETTE® *Desire*®

Do you want...

**D**angerously handsome heroes

**E**vocative, everlasting love stories

**S**izzling and tantalizing sensuality

**I**ncredibly sexy miniseries like **MAN OF THE MONTH**

**R**ed-hot romance

**E**nticing entertainment that can't be beat!

You'll find all of this, and much *more* each and every month in **SILHOUETTE DESIRE**. Don't miss these unforgettable love stories by some of romance's hottest authors. Silhouette Desire—where your fantasies will always come true....

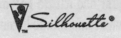

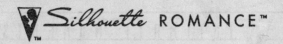
**Silhouette** ROMANCE™

**What's a single dad to do when he needs a wife by next Thursday?**

**Who's a confirmed bachelor to call when he finds a baby on his doorstep?**

**How does a plain Jane in love with her gorgeous boss get him to notice her?**

From classic love stories to romantic comedies to emotional heart tuggers, **Silhouette Romance** offers six irresistible novels every month by some of your favorite authors! Such as...beloved bestsellers **Diana Palmer, Annette Broadrick, Suzanne Carey, Elizabeth August** and **Marie Ferrarella**, to name just a few—and some sure to become favorites!

Fabulous Fathers...Bundles of Joy...Miniseries... Months of blushing brides and convenient weddings... Holiday celebrations... You'll find all this and much more in **Silhouette Romance**—always emotional, always enjoyable, always about love!

# WAYS TO *UNEXPECTEDLY* MEET MR. RIGHT:

♡ Go out with the sexy-sounding stranger your daughter secretly set you up with through a personal ad.

♡ RSVP yes to a wedding invitation—soon it might be your turn to say "I do!"

♡ Receive a marriage proposal by mail— from a man you've never met....

These are just a few of the unexpected ways that written communication leads to love in Silhouette Yours Truly.

Each month, look for two fast-paced, fun and flirtatious Yours Truly novels (with entertaining treats and sneak previews in the back pages) by some of your favorite authors—and some who are sure to become favorites.

## YOURS TRULY™:
Love—when you least expect it!

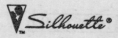

# FIVE UNIQUE SERIES
# FOR EVERY WOMAN YOU ARE...

### ▼ *Silhouette* ROMANCE™

From classic love stories to romantic comedies to emotional heart tuggers, Silhouette Romance is sometimes sweet, sometimes sassy—and always enjoyable! Romance—the way you always knew it could be.

### SILHOUETTE® *Desire*®

Red-hot is what we've got! Sparkling, scintillating, *sensuous* love stories. Once you pick up one you won't be able to put it down...only in Silhouette Desire.

### *Silhouette*® SPECIAL EDITION®

Stories of love and life, these powerful novels are tales that you can identify with—romances with "something special" added in! Silhouette Special Edition is entertainment for the heart.

### SILHOUETTE·INTIMATE·MOMENTS®

Enter a world where passions run hot and excitement is always high. Dramatic, larger than life and always compelling—Silhouette Intimate Moments provides captivating romance to cherish forever.

### ▼ SILHOUETTE YOURS TRULY™

A personal ad, a "Dear John" letter, a wedding invitation... Just a few of the ways that written communication unexpectedly leads Miss Unmarried to Mr. "I Do" in Yours Truly novels...in the most fun, fast-paced and flirtatious style!